T0316214

Bello:
hidden talent rediscovered!

Bello is a digital only imprint of Pan Macmillan,
established to breathe new life into previously published,
classic books.

At Bello we believe in the timeless power of the imagination,
of good story, narrative and entertainment and we want to use
digital technology to ensure that many more readers
can enjoy these books into the future.

We publish in ebook and Print on Demand formats
to bring these wonderful books to new audiences.

About Bello:

www.panmacmillan.com/imprints/bello

About the author:

www.panmacmillan.com/author/andrewgarve

Andrew Garve

Andrew Garve is the pen name of Paul Winterton (1908–2001). He was born in Leicester and educated at the Hulme Grammar School, Manchester and Purley County School, Surrey, after which he took a degree in Economics at London University. He was on the staff of *The Economist* for four years, and then worked for fourteen years for the *London News Chronicle* as reporter, leader writer and foreign correspondent. He was assigned to Moscow from 1942/5, where he was also the correspondent of the BBC's Overseas Service.

After the war he turned to full-time writing of detective and adventure novels and produced more than forty-five books. His work was serialized, televised, broadcast, filmed and translated into some twenty languages. He is noted for his varied and unusual backgrounds – which have included Russia, newspaper offices, the West Indies, ocean sailing, the Australian outback, politics, mountaineering and forestry – and for never repeating a plot.

Andrew Garve was a founder member and first joint secretary of the Crime Writers' Association.

Andrew Garve

MURDERER'S FEN

First published in 1966 by Collins

This edition published 2011 by Bello
an imprint of Pan Macmillan, a division of Macmillan Publishers Limited
Pan Macmillan, 20 New Wharf Road, London N1 9RR
Basingstoke and Oxford
Associated companies throughout the world

www.panmacmillan.com/imprints/bello
www.curtisbrown.co.uk

ISBN 978-1-4472-1528-8 EPUB
ISBN 978-1-4472-1527-1 POD

PART ONE

Chapter One

Alan Hunt lay back in his deck chair above the fiord, bare-chested, browning his splendid, muscular torso in the August sun. He was a big, blond, strikingly handsome man. His age was just short of thirty.

From all around came cheerful holiday sounds—gay laughter, the splash of water, the thud of tennis balls, the putter of outboard motors, the creak of oars. Hunt, having risen early and swum for an hour, had no urge to join in the activity at the moment. But it made a pleasant and soothing background to his thoughts.

Presently, a deeper throb caused him to raise his head. The hotel launch was coming in with a new batch of guests from the mainland. As usual, it was pretty full. The hotel was on the itinerary of many package tours, and as most of the guests stayed only for a day or two there was always a busy two-way traffic across the fiord. This batch seemed much like any other—a lot of young people in lively groups, families with children, a few elderly couples . . . Then, as Hunt lazily looked them over, his eye was caught by a girl—and he suddenly sat up. She was standing between a middle-aged man and woman, pointing something out on the shore. What had caught Hunt's attention was a head of glorious chestnut hair. He had always had a special weakness for redheads of that shade. He wondered what the rest of her would be like. He continued to watch as the launch drew in to the quay and the boatman made it fast.

He could see the girl better, now. As she stepped ashore, he sized up her points with a practised eye. Good legs, smashing figure. Hair wavy, and worn shoulder length. Good carriage, head held up. Medium height, graceful. A youthful twenty, he reckoned . . . Accompanied by parents. . . .

Passing Hunt's chair on the way to the reception desk, she gave him an interested glance. Most girls did . . . At close quarters, she looked even more attractive. Dimples, he noted. Deep blue eyes—wonderful with that hair. Not much make-up but with her complexion and colouring she didn't need much. No ring on her finger. Very fresh-looking. Untouched by hand, Hunt guessed. A succulent dish for someone. But not alas, for him. . . .

He felt more frustrated than ever. Back in the winter, when he'd booked this Norwegian trip, the prospect of a few days on his own at the Vistasund Hotel had seemed inviting. A hotel in a delightful island setting, magnificent seascapes, wonderful smorgasbord, swimming and water-skiing, boats of every kind for the asking, dancing in the evenings—and plenty of girls. Some of them certainly willing. He'd counted on that. Back in the winter, it had been a warming thought . . . But now, in his changed circumstances, it hadn't seemed safe. A holiday affair could have repercussions—and he had too much at stake to risk getting involved . . . So, for nearly a week, he'd had to eye the goods instead of handling them. Not that any of the girls had been particularly inspiring—but one or two had looked possible. It had been a tantalising experience, and an unfamiliar one for Hunt. Probably, he thought, he'd have done better to cancel the trip in the spring, and ask for his money back . . . Still, he'd only another two days to go. He ought to be able to resist temptation for two more days—even with that lovely dish around.

The trouble was that he kept on running into the new girl, and each time he saw her it was like a high-voltage charge going through him.

She was in the lounge with her parents when he went in for an *aquavit* before lunch. They were all drinking orange squash. Dad, at close range, was a tall, spare, greying man in his late fifties—distinguished-looking in an austere sort of way. All his features had a drawn-out look—his high, narrow forehead; his thin

4

nose; his long upper lip, which gave his face a severe and disapproving expression even in repose. He was wearing a dark suit of an old-fashioned cut, complete with waistcoat, and looked more like a chapel sidesman than a holiday-maker. Mum was plump and pleasant-faced, with snowy white hair that might once have been chestnut too. A striking enough pair in their way—but Hunt couldn't help feeling it must have surprised them to produce such a wonder girl.

Mum, it appeared, was inclined to fuss. She was fussing now about the girl's dress—a simple, summer affair in flowered blue linen. Hunt could see nothing wrong with it except that it revealed too little. Presently she started fussing about the funny eiderdowns she'd found on the beds, and wondering how they were going to get any sleep with no sheets or blankets to tuck in. She and Dad both had slight Midland accents. The girl had less of an accent—and less to say. She was, Hunt knew, aware of him. When she caught his eye, she smiled, a little wistfully. She looked as though she'd like to step out and have a bit of fun. "Watch it, boy!" Hunt told himself.

He ran into her again at lunch as she surveyed, with the uncertainty of a newcomer, the magnificent "serve yourself" table that stretched almost the length of the dining-room. "What a lot of things to choose from!" she exclaimed to a woman next to her. "This is nothing," the woman said. "At the last place I was at, we had forty-three different *cold* dishes alone!" Hunt moved in. "I'm an old hand," he said, with a smile. "May I give you the lay-out . . .?" Courtesy and charm were his professional tools. He directed the girl to the fragrant hot dishes at one end of the table—the meat balls and fish balls and fried potatoes and stew; the cold sweets, plates, knives and forks at the other end; the fish dishes and hors d'oeuvres down one side of the board; the breads and cheeses down the other. "That fish in wine sauce is tasty," he said, "and the rissoles in gravy are much better than they sound . . . I don't advise the reindeer—it's like gumboot." The girl laughed, showing pretty teeth.

He saw her again after lunch, though briefly. He was sitting at an umbrella-shaded table in the hotel grounds, drinking coffee and sipping a liqueur, when she came strolling by, flanked by her parents like a prisoner under guard. Dad had got hold of a coloured brochure and was reading aloud about various trips they could take together in the hotel launch. As they drew level, Hunt caught a little of their conversation. The girl said, "What I'd really like to do is go out in one of those little sailing boats." Mum said, "Oh, I don't think I'd do that, dear, they don't look very safe to me." The girl said, "Mum, they're perfectly safe—they're like the one Sally and I took out on the Nene last summer, and I managed all right then." Mum said, "That was a river, dear, and this is almost like the sea." Dad weighed in judiciously. "I'm told the wind gets up very quickly in these fiords . . ." And the voices faded.

Hunt saw her once more that afternoon—out on the water. He was having his second swim of the day when she came rowing by, alone, in one of the hotel's long, viking-type dinghies. Mum and Dad had evidently accepted that as a safe compromise—though they were watching her closely from deck chairs on the shore. The girl rowed well, Hunt saw. He also noticed that she had shapely arms, sun-tanned to a delicate gold, and thought how nice it would be if she were like that all over. She gave him a little smile of recognition as she passed. A charming smile, showing her dimples, but without self-consciousness, without coquetry. Just friendly . . . Hunt called out, "I'll race you," and went into a powerful crawl. For thirty yards he kept abreast of her. Then he laughed, and waved, and dropped back. It would be so easy to start something with her—and it was so tempting. But it really wouldn't do. . . .

There was the usual lively dance session after dinner. The dancing took place on the cleared floor of the dining-room, where there was space for fifty couples—a gleaming area of polished pine much mutilated by stiletto heels. There were records for everyone's taste, and most of the guests joined in. Those who preferred to watch sat in the lounge, which was on a higher level and railed off, like a ship's quarterdeck. It was there, Hunt noticed, that the new girl was sitting with her parents, hemmed in by people, inaccessible without disturbance. There was no "Keep Off " sign, but the message was clear. It wasn't the girl's message, though—Hunt was sure of that. She hadn't put on a dress of midnight blue velvet to sit with Mum and Dad all evening. He decided to try for one dance. He'd danced with almost all the available girls at one time or another, distributing his favours evenly—so why not with the redhead? He waited for a waltz—there was nothing like a waltz for close work. Then, with quiet assurance, he made his way through the lounge, bowed to the parents, and asked the girl if she would dance. She glanced at her father before getting up, as though seeking permission. Dad looked at Hunt for a moment, then gave an Olympian nod. Hunt led the girl down to the dance floor and steered her quickly and skilfully to the far end of the room, where they were masked by other dancers.

"Having fun?" he asked her.

"I am now" she said, smiling.

Hunt looked down at her. She had a vivid mouth, barely touched with lipstick. Her hair smelt delicious. She danced with natural grace. Her body was firm, yet pliant. Her very simplicity was exciting. She was like a flower that hadn't opened. A beauty unaware of her own attraction.

"What's your name?" Hunt asked.

"Gwenda Nicholls."

"Gwenda . . .? M'm—I like that. It's unusual . . . Mine's Alan Hunt."

She nodded. "Have you been here long?"

"About a week."

"Oh . . . Then I suppose you'll be leaving soon."

"In a couple of days."

She was silent for a moment "It's a lovely place, isn't it?"

"Pretty good, yes."

"It's the loveliest place I've ever been in. All the colours, and the different lights—and everything so peaceful. I think it's heaven."

"It's certainly fun being on an island," Hunt said. "You probably haven't seen much of it yet . . . There are lots of little winding paths through the heather, most of them ending in rocky coves."

"How lovely—I'm dying to explore . . . It's all so different from what I'm used to."

"What are you used to?"

"Brickworks and chimneys, mostly. I don't mean we live among them, but you can always see them . . . I live in Peterborough—Dad works in the Council offices . . . Have you ever been there?"

"I think I drove through it once."

"That's the best thing to do with it," she said. "I hate all towns—I don't know how people can bear them . . . If I ever get the chance I shall live in the country."

"What do you do in Peterborough?"

She made a face. "I'm a shorthand typist."

"Don't you like it?"

"Not much . . . I work in a solicitor's office, and it's rather dull. There's just me and Miss Harris—she's a middle-aged woman who's been there donkey's years—and we hardly see a soul."

"Why don't you change to something else?"

"Well, I have thought of it, but the solicitor's a friend of Dad's, and Mum likes it because the office isn't too far away and I can go home for lunch . . . What do *you* do?"

"I'm a salesman," Hunt said.

"What do you sell?"

"I've sold practically everything in my time. It's caravans, at the moment."

She nodded. "I should think you'd be rather a good salesman."

"What makes you say that?"

"Well, you've got the right sort of voice—quiet, and sort of coaxing."

He laughed. It was on the tip of his tongue to say, "Can I coax you?"—but he thought better of it. No point in a neat gambit when there was no chance of a follow-up. "Maybe you're right," he said. "Anyway, I get by."

"You're on your own here, aren't you?" "Yes."

Gwenda glanced across at Mum and Dad.

"I wish *I* was."

The music stopped. Hunt gave the girl's body a slight squeeze, and released her. "Thank you," he said. "That was most enjoyable."

He took her back to where her parents were sitting. Gwenda introduced him. He made polite conversation for a moment or two—about the hotel, the island, the trips. Then he asked to be excused.

Well, that's it, he told himself. That's about the ration. It was a shame, because the girl had obviously taken to him—and she'd make a delicious snack. But all the signals were at danger. She was inexperienced, romantic, probably longing for a steady boy friend. Mum was probably looking for a son-in-law. Dad certainly wasn't the man to see his daughter trifled with. Both were watchful. It just wouldn't do. Prudence, boy, prudence! And maybe a cold shower . . . After all, there were lots of lovely women in the world—and in a few months, with luck, he'd be able to take his pick. . . .

He had a couple of drinks in the bar and an interesting chat with a man from Leeds who said he'd won thirteen thousand pounds on the pools a year ago and had since turned it into eighteen thousand. Hunt was always fascinated by money and what you could do with it—especially money that hadn't been earned by hard work. He talked and listened for half an hour, picking up several useful tips. Then he went upstairs to write a letter.

His room, like all the single ones, was on the top floor of the building, at the back. It was small but comfortable, with a well-sprung bed, a writing-table, an easy-chair and plenty of reading-lamps. The daytime view from the window, over calm fiords and low, purple islands, was superb. After dark, a luminous glow from the water still gave a sense of space. Hunt opened the french doors and stepped out on to his little iron balcony, sniffing the fragrant air. The sky, he saw, had become overcast, but the night was pleasantly mild. Quiet, too, except for the strains of music coming from the dining-room below. The dancing usually went on till after midnight, and the time was still only a little after ten.

He was about to go back in and start his letter when a light clicked on in the room next door and a girl came out on to the neighbouring balcony. Even in the shadows, he recognised her at once. It was Gwenda Nicholls.

"Well, hallo again," he said. He didn't have to raise his voice—the ends of the balconies were only a few feet apart. "I'd no idea we were neighbours."

"Nor had I," she said. She didn't look at all displeased.

"You've left the dancing early."

"Mum was tired after the journey—she's taken Dad off to bed."

"So you had to come to bed too?"

She hesitated. "Well, in a way ... They don't really like me dancing. Especially if they're not there to keep an eye on me."

"You're not serious?"

"I'm afraid so. My parents are Baptists, you see—not the strictest sort but—well, old-fashioned about things ... Dad's very keen on temperance, and not playing games on Sundays—he's always writing letters to the papers about it ... He doesn't actually stop me dancing, but he doesn't really approve."

Hunt tut-tutted. "How old are you, for heaven's sake?"

"I was twenty last week."

"It's fantastic. In this day and age."

"That's what I think. I keep telling them I'm much too old to be treated like a child."

"Can't you do anything about it? Talk them round?"

"Well, I do try—we have terrible arguments at home ... Rows, almost ... The thing is, I'm really fond of them and I know they're fond of me—so it's difficult. They honestly think I still need looking after and protecting ... But I get very fed up, always being asked where I'm going and what I'm going to do and who with and having to be in by ten o'clock and all the rest of the stupid rules ... After all, most girls of my age do pretty well as they like, don't they?"

"They certainly do," Hunt said.

"Mum's the worst—she will go on at me all the time. We get on each other's nerves like anything ... I think we'd both be better off if I left home and got a job somewhere else, but she won't hear of it. I will in the end, I'm sure, but it'll take some doing ... What I really want to do is go and look after children in the country."

"Sounds a jolly good idea," Hunt said—though he couldn't have cared less about her future. He was much more interested now in her present. It had dawned on him, while she'd been talking, that the fates had played straight into his hands and that he needn't resist temptation any more. All the omens had suddenly become favourable. By a wonderful stroke of luck he'd been given a room adjacent to hers, both of them with balconies; the ideal set-up for a safe and secret intrigue, a Casanova's dream. The girl was in a state of near-rebellion over her "lock up your daughter" parents, so she wasn't at all likely to blab. She was venturesome, eager for a fling, thirsting for experience—and she liked him . . . The perfect frame of mind . . . And in less than a couple of days he was due to leave. It should be a cinch.

He thought so even more a few minutes later, when it began to rain.

"Blast!" he said. "Now we'll have to go in . . . Just when we were getting to know each other."

Gwenda looked disappointed, too.

"Anyway," he said, "I really ought to write a letter. . . ." But he didn't move.

Neither did Gwenda. "I suppose you're writing to your girl friend," she said,

He shook his head. "No such luck . . . To my mother."

"You mean you haven't got a girl friend?"

"Not so far . . . I guess I'm too choosy . . . Look, you're getting awfully wet, you really ought to go in."

"I suppose so . . ."

He half turned—then stopped, as though a thought had suddenly occurred to him. "Of course, I could step across to your balcony and we could go on talking inside . . . But perhaps you wouldn't like that." Gwenda looked at the gap—and at the ground, forty feet below. "You wouldn't dare."

"Who wouldn't?—I'd be over in a jiffy . . . Still, I'm sure your parents wouldn't approve. I'd better write my letter."

Gwenda hesitated. "You really think it's safe?"

Hunt eyed the gap. It was well over four feet across—a long stride. But he'd never been averse from taking a calculated risk if the prize was tempting enough. "Piece of cake," he said.

"Well—all right . . . Just for a minute."

"Is your door locked?"

"Yes."

Hunt glanced down, and to right and left. The rain had driven everyone indoors; there was no one in sight. "Here I come, then . . ." He swung a leg over the side of the balcony, then the other. For a moment he stood poised on the ledge, looking at Gwenda, smiling. Then, with a long, measured leap, he gained a foothold and grabbed the rail of Gwenda's balcony at the same instant. She gave a gasp of relief as he climbed over. "Easy," he said—though it hadn't been. He followed her into her room. It was a replica of his own, except that everything was arranged the other way round

He grinned at her. "I bet you've never done anything like this before," he said.

She shook her head. "I certainly haven't And considering we only met to-day, it seems a bit crazy"

"But that's what makes it such fun, don't you think? Anyway, one can live a lifetime in a day." Hunt swivelled the soft chair round for her, and seated himself on the hard one. "How I wish you'd come here a week ago."

"Do you?"

"It would have made all the difference to me, I can tell you . . . Of course, there's been plenty to do—I won't pretend it's been dull . . . But having someone around that one likes is what really matters."

"I thought a lot of the girls here looked very attractive."

"H'm . . . Not by my standards—especially now I've met you. You're terrific—do you know that . . .? But I'm not talking about looks, I'm talking about liking . . . Somehow, you're different—I don't know what it is. I thought so the moment you came off the boat. The way you walked, the way you hold your head—everything about you . . . It's personality, I suppose."

"You're not exactly short of personality yourself," Gwenda said, the dimples appearing.

"Well, I hope I'm not . . . Tell me, what are you planning to do to-morrow?"

"I think we're going on the round trip in the launch."

"Oh . . ." Hunt pretended to be disappointed—though it suited him very well. The less he saw of her publicly from now on, the better. "In that case," he said, "I think I'll fix up to do some fishing . . . But we'll have some time together to-morrow evening, won't we?"

"We could . . ."

"And perhaps we could see some more of each other when we get home? I move around quite a bit in my job—I could easily look in at Peterborough. If you'd like me to, that is."

"It would be rather nice."

"I'll write my address down and give it to you before I go . . . Heavens, just listen to that rain!"

"Oughtn't you to go back before it gets worse?"

"Yes, perhaps I'd better . . ." He'd prepared the ground now—there was no point in staying longer. If they went on talking, the girl would probably want to know more about him, which would mean a lot of tedious invention . . . He got up, stretching out his hands and drawing Gwenda up too. "You are so pretty," he said. "Would it be taking advantage of you if I kissed you good night?"

She smiled. "I don't think so."

He took her in his arms and kissed her mouth. She kissed him back—tentatively at first, then with growing passion. His appetite for her sharpened—but prudence held him back. At this rate, to-morrow would arrive to-night!—and she wasn't ready for the whole works yet. Besides, it would mean a day of danger before he left. He drew away, gazed for a moment into her eyes, tenderly touched her hair. Overcome, it seemed, by an emotion he found it hard to express. "You're sweet," he said. "Really sweet . . . Good night, darling. Sleep well."

"Be careful," she whispered after him.

He looked out cautiously. All was quiet, except for the downpour. The gap he had to cross was uninviting now, but he didn't hesitate. If he broke his neck, he thought wryly, it would be in a good cause. He climbed the rail, measured the distance, braced himself—and in one long stride he was safely back. From his balcony, he blew a farewell kiss to Gwenda. Inside the bedroom, he grinned cheerfully to himself. Everything had gone according to his expectations. The girl, unnaturally deprived of male company and eager for love, had already fallen for him. He'd swept her off her feet—practically hypnotised her with his assurance and charm. And because he'd behaved well, she'd have no reason to distrust him to-morrow. It *was* going to be a cinch.

He still had his letter to write. He sat down now at the table and quickly dashed it off. It ran:

Dearest Susan,

Only another two days and I'll be on my way back to you! I can't tell you how I'm counting the hours. I've missed you terribly, darling, every minute of the time. This hotel isn't a bad place and the scenery is grand, but I find myself mooning about thinking of you and not really wanting to talk to anyone, which you'll agree isn't like me. I suppose it's just a part of being in love—not being interested in anyone else. The truth is that nothing's the same without you. I keep thinking what a wonderful time we could have had here together, swimming and boating and sunning ourselves and living the kind of active, outdoor life we both like so much. It seems a real shame that you couldn't come, though I do see one can't take a new job and then immediately ask for a holiday. But with luck this will be the last time we'll be separated, darling. What a marvellous thought!

I hope you got all my earlier letters. I picked your last one up at Stavanger and I laughed no end at your description of the Rally. You really are a bit of a madcap. Yes, I remember old Carson. Isn't he the chap who hit a tree while he was fastening his safety belt?

I'll ring you the moment I get back. What I'd really like to do is catch a plane—but I suppose that would be extravagant. I'm sure your father would think so. Please give him my warm regards, and your mother. I hope her sciatica is better.

All my love, darling—and see you soon.

Alan

Before he turned in, Hunt went downstairs and posted the letter in the hotel box. One way and another, he thought, it had been a well-spent evening.

The skies had cleared by morning. The fiord was blue again, the sun warm and bright. Hunt made a point of going down late to breakfast, to give time for the launch party to leave on their all-day trip before he showed himself.

He spent the morning swmiming and sun-bathing with a gay group at the diving-board. In the afternoon he borrowed a rod and a boat and went fishing in the Sound. He was around when the launch party got back at five o'clock, and he gave Gwenda a little wave and a conspiratorial smile as she came ashore. At dinner he stopped for a moment by the Nichollses' table and asked politely if they'd had a good day. After dinner he allowed himself one dance with Gwenda, holding her close to him, telling her how pretty she looked and how much he liked her dress, gazing meaningfully into her eyes, softening her up. He'd see her later, he whispered, as they separated—and her eager nod told him that she'd been thinking of little else all day. Afterwards he danced with several other girls, just to show that he wasn't singling anyone out Then he retired to the bar to plan his final tactics. He'd never felt in a better mood. He was thoroughly enjoying the excitement of the chase and the challenge of the hazards.

It was shortly before eleven when he crossed to Gwenda's room. At once he took her into his arms. "It's been such a long, long day," he said. Gwenda sighed, and nestled against him. She didn't seem at all nervous about having him there. Just happy. . . .

She looked even happier when, a few minutes later, he produced a piece of paper with his address on it—Flat 5, Esmeralda House, Brighton. "Do write to me when you get home, won't you?" he said. "And I'll write to you. What's your address?" He jotted it down on an old envelope—19 Everton Road, Peterborough. "Good . . . And I'll get up there as soon as I can."

They sat on the bed then, and kissed, and talked. Hushed, delightful talk—but mostly kisses. Hunt saw how Gwenda's eyes kept searching his, as though she couldn't believe that this miracle was happening to her. Yes, she'd fallen for him, all right.

Suddenly he said, "Why, I was almost forgetting—I brought something along to celebrate with ...." He fished a small bottle out of his pocket. "Gin and Italian—I got them to mix it at the bar. I hope you like it."

"I don't think I ever tried it," Gwenda said. "I hardly ever drink ... Dad would be furious."

"Well, he's not here now, and you're a big girl. ... We'll have to take turns with your tooth glass, I'm afraid." He fetched the glass, and poured a drink for her.

She tried it, cautiously. "It's a bit strong," she said. "It's nice, though."

"I thought you'd like it. Leave me a drop, will you ..." She laughed and handed him the glass, which he refilled.

"You know," he said, "it's going to seem a very empty world to-morrow. Especially to-morrow night. I'll be thinking of you, alone here ..." Tenderly, he stroked her hair. "I do believe I've fallen in love with you."

"Alan, you can't have ... It's absurd."

"Why—because we only met yesterday? People do, you know—love at first sight. It often happens—and I think it's quite the most romantic way ... What about you, Gwenda? You like me a bit, don't you?"

"You know I do ... I wish you weren't going."

"Let's not think about that. Let's think how wonderful it will be when we see each other again. Let's think of the future. ..." He poured more drink into the glass. "Here's a toast—to our next meeting, and may it be soon!"

They drank in turn, kissing between sips. When the drink was all gone they kissed again, clinging together in a long and passionate embrace.

"You're lovely," Hunt said. He drew her down beside him. "So warm, so soft. ... I'd like to stay like this with you. I'd like to be with you for ever ..."

He sought her mouth again. His hand strayed over her breasts.

She shivered, clinging to him. The hand strayed further. "No," she said, "no . . ."

"But darling . . . I love you."

"No. . . . Oh, Alan, don't . . ."

"I'll be careful—ever so careful. Gwenda, I love you—I really do . . . I want you . . ."

For a moment, she fought him. Hunt's hand was ready to move, to clamp down brutally on her mouth if necessary, stifling any scream. But it wasn't necessary. The old magic worked. With a sigh that was half a sob, she relaxed.

They said their private good-byes in the morning, across the gap of the balconies. Gwenda was subdued, a little shy, a little lost in a new world—but not unhappy. Hunt said the right things. He loved her deeply, he'd soon be writing to her, they'd soon be meeting. He could hardly wait for the day. . . . Then, as though with a great effort, he tore himself away.

He packed quickly, and carried his bag to the quay. Gwenda was already there. He put the bag down with the luggage of the other passengers, and went into the office to pay his bill.

When he returned, Gwenda had disappeared. The boatman was waiting to cast off the ropes. There were a dozen other passengers travelling, and the usual knot of guests to wave them good-bye. Hunt went aboard. He could see Gwenda's father in the crowd, but there was still no sign of Gwenda. Perhaps, Hunt thought, she'd found the actual parting more of an ordeal than she could face. Anyway, it didn't matter. It was all over now. She could write to Flat 5, Esmeralda House, till her arm dropped off, but the letters would never be delivered—since, as far as Hunt knew, there wasn't such a place.

It had been a good trip, after all. One more attractive virgin notched up—and a clean getaway.

Chapter Two

The one true thing Hunt had told Gwenda Nicholls was that he was a salesman—and the one sound judgment she'd made of him was that he was good at it. He'd been selling things on commission since he was eighteen, and as it was work for which his sharp wits, persuasiveness and charm equipped him well, he'd prospered without too much effort. Some of his talent might have been inherited—his father had sold advertising space for a weekly magazine with success and profit until his death a few years earlier. But whereas Hunt senior had been a diligent and conscientious man who had worked for the same firm for most of his life, his son had turned out a pleasure-loving drifter. Alan Hunt had long ago decided that there was no big money in salesmanship without much more application than he was prepared to give. So he'd looked around for a short cut to easy wealth—and recently he'd found it.

His lack of principle and scruple, his ruthless unconcern about what he did to other people, his total inability to feel affection or tenderness for anyone, could not be explained or excused by any reference to his early background. He had not been brought up in a slum, he had not been a latch-key child, he had not been deprived of love or made to feel inferior. He had not come from a broken home—his parents had been devoted to each other. In childhood, he had been neither pampered nor neglected. He had been sent, at a normal age, to a sound if minor public school, where he had made friends in a normal way and appeared perfectly happy. He had done well at games, shown an aptitude for mathematics and particularly mathematical puzzles, and distinguished himself in amateur theatricals. The school, on his departure, had been warm in his praise. "A good all-rounder, whom we shall miss," his last report had said. "Should do well in whatever career he chooses."

There was, in fact, no discernible reason why Hunt had turned out as he had except that by some untraceable genetic mischance he'd been fated to mature that way. At thirty, he was a living disproof of the facile view that there is some good in everyone. Hunt was bad right through.

For the past few months he had been in sole charge of a sales depot, near the village of Ocken in Cambridgeshire, for a company called Cosy Caravans which had its headquarters in Ipswich. His main job at Ocken was to receive potential customers attracted by display advertisements in the newspapers; show them over the available stock, and persuade them to buy. He also had to accept and dispatch vans according to instructions from head office, maintain various stores, and keep on top of the paper work. As a sideline, profitable to himself as well as to the company, he was required to keep an eye on a number of private motor cruisers moored along the left bank of the drain or "lode" that formed one boundary of the property.

The job had proved moderately lucrative during the summer months, when commissions had been good. The firm had had to be generous about money, because of the difficulty of getting anyone suitable to take on the position at all. It was virtually a one-man post and, except when customers called, there was little companionship. The village itself was no more than a developed hamlet on a main road, and lacked communal life. The caravan site, lying back from the road and approached by its own drive, was lonely. The amenities were few. The only buildings were a small wooden office, with a table, chair, filing cabinet and telephone, and a larger shed for stores. Because the firm liked to have someone there all the time to keep watch on the thirty or forty caravans and the boats, Hunt had to live and look after himself in one of the vans.

The view from the site was, in his opinion, exceptionally dreary.

A nature reserve extended for hundreds of acres—a flat, windswept area of fen that in part had never been reclaimed and in part had remained uncultivated since ancient times. It consisted in the main of swampy reeds and sedge, black earth and peat, pools, dykes, drains and droves. Except for two wooden towers—an old, near-derelict hide for observing wild life and a new one built alongside it—it had no prominent features. Ocken Fen was famous among naturalists; and popular in summer with anglers and people who enjoyed strolling along quiet paths in an unspoilt setting. Lovers found it very handy, too. For Hunt it was an eyesore—useful for exercise, but depressing to look at. In fact, he loathed the place … All the same, he'd gladly taken the job, and he'd been very satisfied with it. It had served him well …

Everything seemed in good order when he got back to the site on the second Saturday in August. He was greeted by Taylor, his holiday deputy from head office, a young man with a black beard so carefully shaped and pruned that it looked like an experiment in topiary. Taylor was in high good humour, having sold three vans in ten days. But he was also quite ready to leave. "Dead-and-alive hole, I call this," he said. "Specially at night. … I'd go bonkers if I had to stay long."

"You've got to have inner resources," Hunt said, grinning. "Philosophical disposition—love of nature in the raw. … Like me …" He was feeling pretty cheerful himself. "Anyway, how were things? Any problems?"

"Not really," Taylor said. "Joe hurt his leg, but he's getting better." Joe was a villager with a Land-Rover, who sometimes delivered vans for the firm. "We've had two more applications for boat berths for the winter—the letters are on the file. The bottled gas came, and the paraffin's coming next week. Ipswich sent a few stores—they're in the shed. Oh, and I fixed up with a bloke named Ellis to see you at eleven o'clock on Monday morning—he's interested in the Midgets, and sounds a good prospect. That's about all."

Hunt nodded. "You seem to have coped all right." He glanced

through the correspondence and accounts. "Did you order the milk and groceries I asked for?"

"Yes, they're in the van."

"Good ... You can push off, then, if you like."

"Thanks, Mr. Hunt ... Did you have a good holiday?"

"A splendid holiday," Hunt said, with a reminiscent gleam.

He watched Taylor drive away on his motor-bike. Then he set off on a round of the site. It was a large area—perhaps a quarter of a mile long by a hundred yards wide—with a shallow S-bend in the middle. It had once been an arable field and the surface, now grassed down, was still a little irregular. The office and shed were close together near the entrance. From there, four rows of new caravans stretched away down the centre, suitably spaced. Hunt's van was the last on the right and was set a little apart from the others, close to the water. On the north boundary of the site, a screen of dark conifers gave protection and privacy. On the south side was the lode, with the fen beyond. The lode looked like a natural river, though according to the experts it had been dug centuries ago for drainage purposes and for the local transport of peat and sedge. It was twenty yards wide, with willow-lined banks, and it flowed at a barely perceptible pace to join the rest of the fen waterways network lower down.

Even on this high-season Saturday, the place was very quiet. Only two of the long line of moored boats appeared to be occupied for the week-end. Hunt paused briefly to exchange greetings with their respective owners, and to eye a bikini-clad figure on a cabin top. A boy asked him if he had a woolly cap in the store, and he said he'd look. Continuing along the bank towards his van, he noticed that the mahogany rowing dinghy he sometimes used to cross the lode had more water in it than usual. There must have been a lot of rain in his absence—though the ground looked dry enough now. He stopped by his car, a cream MG sports to which he was very attached, and removed the polythene cover. The car appeared to have taken no harm. He looked inside his van, found it stuffy, and opened a couple of windows. He was about to put his groceries away when the telephone bell rang. in the office—a specially loud one he'd had fitted so that he could hear it anywhere on the site. He walked back and answered a query from Ipswich.

Then he rang up Susan.

He met her that evening by arrangement at the Crown Hotel, Newmarket, where for some weeks she had been working "for fun" as a receptionist. Her greeting in the foyer as she came off duty was deceptively casual—she had no taste for public demonstrations. "Let's go to Hayes Corner," she said. They drove, in their separate cars and at a dangerously high speed, to the quiet, wooded spot on the way to Susan's home which they'd often used as a necking place. There, Hunt joined her in her Austin Healey, and they twined around each other in passionate but innocent reunion, kissing and murmuring endearments. Hunt never attempted anything more with Susan. Apart from the fact that he didn't much want to, he had his image to think of. The image of a considerate, reliable, thoroughly decent bloke whose passions would remain well under control until the parson gave the "off." If Susan wanted more, as he guessed she did, she had only to name the date.

Susan Ainger was twenty-two. She was a tall girl, with nondescript-coloured hair, a jolly laugh, a plain face and almost no figure. She made the best of herself, wearing clothes that were both expensive and attractive, and having her hair done regularly in Cambridge, but no one would ever have called her an eyeful. She was moderately intelligent, but her academic knowledge was minuscule. She had gained little from her exclusive boarding school education except social know-how and an accent that fell pleasantly on the ear.

She was an only child, and rather a spoiled one. Strong-minded and independent by nature, she had been allowed to do pretty much as she liked. What she had mainly liked, until now, had been physical and extrovert—driving and dancing, galloping on the Heath, swimming and tennis, and generally having a good time with young companions who regarded her as a good pal. Recently, her interests had become more mature. She was fundamentally a warm-hearted and affectionate girl with normal instincts, and she wanted to love

22

a man and be loved by him, to make a home and have a family. She knew she was no beauty, and she'd wondered sometimes if men would ever regard her as anything but just a good pal. Then she'd met Alan Hunt—handsome, debonair, charming—and soon, miraculously, asking her to marry him. She'd responded to his fervour with warmth and gratitude. Her feeling for him now was the strongest emotion she had ever known.

Chatting freely, they exchanged their news. Both of them were lively talkers. Hunt, as he always did with Susan, made a special effort to be interesting and amusing. It didn't seem likely that at this stage she'd get bored with him and change her mind about marriage, but he didn't believe in relaxing the pressure till he'd reached the post. He told her more about his Norwegian holiday, picking out the oddities that had struck him, running the place down a little since she hadn't been there to enjoy it with him. A lovely country, he said, but you got boiled potatoes with everything, and people hardly ever smiled, and there were no pubs—just men sitting alone at separate tables in dark-panelled restaurants, sipping pots of beer in silence. He produced, as a present for her and to amuse her, one of the grotesque little trolls the Norwegians made such a feature of in their shops, and said with a grin that it reminded him of his boss.

Susan, in turn, told him. about her rally escapade, when she'd had trouble with a police car in a quiet village at midnight; and of an even more exciting episode when her mare, Lady, had got out of the paddock. "There was a weak spot in the hedge," she said, "and I suppose there was better grass outside. Anyway, she walked through into the garden and all over the lawns, and the ground was so soft after the rain, her hoof marks were inches deep. Keller had to go round and patch every hole separately, and do you know, there were two hundred and thirty of them!—it took him days. Daddy was absolutely furious—honestly, I thought he was going to explode. Now he says he's going to put Lady on a ball and chain. . . . !"

Hunt laughed appreciatively. He was always appreciative when

Susan told her light-hearted stories—just as he was always attentive when she was serious. It required a little effort, since he was quite indifferent to her, but it paid off.

Companionably, he held and fondled her left hand as they talked. The ring on it, with its solitaire diamond, had cost him far more than he could afford, but he regarded it as bread upon the waters which would return to him soon. The question was, how soon?

"When are we going to get married?" he asked her, as their flow of chatter momentarily dried up.

She looked up at him, smiling. "As far as I'm concerned," she said, "as soon as you like."

"Darling . . . !" He bent and kissed her. "What about your parents?"

"Well, Mummy still says we haven't known each other long enough, but she's coming round . . . She'll need time to make the arrangements, that's all. She'll want to do everything properly."

"Of course she will. . . . That's all the more reason to get something fixed. How about raising it with them again this evening?"

"All right," Susan said. "Let's."

The Aingers lived in an imposing, neo-Georgian house standing in extensive grounds on the outskirts of the village of Lingford, three miles from Newmarket. It had a sweeping drive-in, a beautifully laid-out garden with some fine old trees, a paddock at the back, and—tidily tucked away behind a macrocarpa hedge—a cottage for a man and wife. There was a servant problem of sorts, but it hadn't been acute since a couple named Keller had been imported from Austria.

Susan put her car in the garage beside her father's Silver Wraith and her mother's Mini, and Hunt parked his in the drive. Then they walked over to where both parents were sitting in the shade of a great copper beech. Mrs. Ainger was a tall, thin woman of fifty with a quiet, genteel voice and a faded prettiness. Hunt greeted her with a kiss on the cheek—his practice since his formal engagement to Susan—and asked her how she was. "Much better, thank you, Alan," she said.

Hunt extended his hand to Ainger. "Hallo, sir." Ainger took it cordially. "Have a good holiday, son?"

"Not too bad," Hunt said. "It would have been better if Susan had been there, of course."

"You'll have enough of her before you've finished," Ainger said with a chuckle.

Henry Ainger was no ordinary man. In appearance he was short and stocky, with powerful shoulders and a tough, craggy face etched with the lines of struggle. He had started life with few assets but his own combative personality. Now, at fifty-eight, he was a minor property tycoon. He had wide interests, splendid health and a tremendous zest for living. With his own family he was usually tolerant and amiable, a dynamo temporarily at rest. In the world of business he was outspoken, ruthless and formidable.

He had not lightly accepted Alan Hunt as his prospective son-in-law. On the contrary, he had weighed him with the care that the special circumstances demanded. He had even had inquiries made about him. He had turned up nothing to cause anxiety, nothing to his discredit. He had checked up on his family background and found it satisfactory. He had looked into some of his past jobs, discussed his work and interests with him, and concluded that he was an able and intelligent fellow. A bit lazy, maybe, a bit too easygoing—but marriage and responsibility would probably change that. Anyway, very ambitious men didn't necessarily make the best husbands. On the personal side, he had no serious criticisms. His wife might be right in thinking he wasn't quite a gentleman—but then neither was Ainger himself. The fellow was presentable, well-mannered, excellent company—and, most important of all, he appeared to be genuinely devoted to Susan. She could certainly have done a lot worse. Ainger's affection for his only daughter didn't blind him to the fact that she wasn't every man's cup of tea. It was unfortunate, but as far as looks were concerned she'd taken after him rather than Jane. She was a nice girl, but she lacked her mother's sweetness and gentle appeal . . . In any case, she'd made up her mind about Alan—and Ainger knew that Susan's mind, in its youthful way, was as tough as his own . . . Having, as he thought, sized the situation up, it was characteristic of him that he accepted it wholeheartedly. Alan would soon be joining the family, and that was that. . . .

He glanced at his watch. "Seven o'clock, eh? Time to bring out the martinis." He set off towards the house.

Susan called after him, "Sherry for me, please," and he waved an acknowledgment. Hunt fetched two more deck chairs from the loggia and placed them under the tree. The sun was still pleasantly warm, the newly-mown lawn fragrant, the surroundings delightful. Gracious living, he thought. Wonderful. There was nothing like affluence. . . .

Mrs. Ainger said, "Do tell me about your holiday, Alan,"—and once more he began to talk about Norway.

Ainger was back in a few minutes with a silver cocktail shaker, a sherry decanter, and four glasses, on a tray. He poured the drinks and passed them round. "Well—it's nice that we're all together again," he said, raising his glass to the company.

Susan took a sip of sherry. "Alan and I would like to get married," she announced.

Mrs. Ainger looked a bit startled. "When, dear?"

"We thought before Christmas."

"So soon. . . .? Isn't that rushing things a little?"

"Oh, Mummy, of course it's not. It's four months. . . . It'll seem ages, anyway."

"Well, Susan, it's your decision, of course—yours and Alan's—but you will have had rather a short engagement. . . ."

"How long were you and Daddy engaged?"

Mrs. Ainger glanced at her husband. Ainger gave a loud guffaw. "No comment," he said.

"There you are, he daren't say. . . . I'll bet it was about a fortnight."

"I think they should fix it, Jane," Ainger said. "They know how they feel—what's the point of hanging about?"

For a moment, Mrs. Ainger said nothing. Then she smiled at Susan. "Very well, dear. . . . Then we'd better start planning."

The next few weeks were among the longest in Hunt's life. To him, they were the gap between the cup and the lip, and he could hardly wait to close it. But he showed nothing of his impatience—except privately to Susan, who was gratified by his eagerness. With her parents, he remained calm, considerate and amenable. He fell in readily with every suggestion they made, as long as Susan agreed. He gave them a potted life history of the best man he had in mind, a former schoolfellow named Roger Lawson. He interested himself in the list of wedding guests and added enough names of his own, but not too many. He had few available relatives, his own parents being dead and his only brother in Canada, but there were a couple of uncles, and an aunt he thought he could rustle up, and he had plenty of friends. His side of the aisle would be respectably filled.

Among the important matters that had to be settled was the question of his job, since it was clear that he couldn't go on living in a caravan and working at Ocken after he was married. He discussed the position with Susan, and then with his firm, who were very accommodating. They had, they said, a high regard for him, and would be happy to give him a post in the sales department at their head office in Ipswich. Hunt reported this to the Aingers one evening in September. Susan, who didn't much mind where she started her married life as long as it was with Alan, thought Ipswich would be fine. Mrs. Ainger agreed that it wasn't too far away from Newmarket and was sure they'd be able to find a nice house there. Ainger listened to the discussion, but said nothing.

Later in the evening, he took Hunt aside. "This business of your job, son," he said. "I've been thinking about it. . . . I'd like to see you getting into something more substantial—something that would stretch your abilities a bit more. . . . Now I could probably find you something in London, where you'd be at the centre of things. A job with real prospects . . . What do you say?"

Hunt hesitated. "That's good of you, sir . . . I appreciate it . . ."

"But . . .?"

"Well, I think my firm has prospects, too . . . Of course, I realise that by your standards it's pretty small stuff—but caravans *are* getting more popular every year, and the firm's doing extremely well. It nearly doubled its profits last year—and it jacked up its dividend by five per cent. . . ."

"Yes, I know," Ainger said, smiling. "I checked."

"So it's going ahead."

"And you think you'll go ahead with it?"

"I think there's a good chance. They seem to like me—and I hear they'll be needing a new sales manager soon. The present one's over sixty and due for retirement. . . . I'd like to give it a try, anyway."

Ainger still looked doubtful. "My guess is it'll never be anything more than a small provincial company. Not under its present management. . . . There won't be much scope there."

"Well, we'll have to see," Hunt said. "Maybe later on I'll take you up on your offer, if it still stands. But not now. . . . After all, the firm *has* just shown its confidence in me—so I feel I owe them a bit of loyalty. Fair's fair. . . . And to be honest, sir, I'm rather keen to start my married life as an independent bloke—even if things don't work out quite so well financially. Matter of pride, I suppose. . . . I hope you understand."

Ainger gave his shoulder a friendly pat. "You bet I understand—in your place I'm sure I'd feel the same. . . . All right, we'll forget it. Come and join me in a glass of port."

By the first Saturday in October, the season at the caravan site was coming to an end. Trade inquiries would go on, but it was unlikely there would be many more private customers until the spring. Most of the boats had been laid up for the winter. Hunt felt less tied to the place than he had been.

That morning at Ocken was a splendid one. After two nights of heavy rain the weather had suddenly become warm and golden and the forecasters were prophesying a spell of Indian summer ahead. Hunt was in the highest spirits. The wedding day was now only eight weeks off. In two months' time he'd be honeymooning in Marrakesh, a safely married man not to be put asunder. After that, things would begin to *move*. He'd be cautious at first, of course. He'd play his hand with subtlety and restraint. There'd be no crude grabbing—just affectionate erosion. A joint bank account would be the thing—showing trust in each other. Naturally, he'd keep in with Ainger. Probably he *would* take up the old boy's offer. Once safely married, there'd be no further reason why he shouldn't—the gesture of independence would have served its purpose. He and Susan would move to London—maybe buy a little mews house in Mayfair, with space underneath for an Aston Martin or an Alfa Romeo. It would be easier for him to organise his bits of fun on the quiet in London. ... Then they'd travel, of course—always in the greatest comfort ... After all, it was up to him to see that Susan wasn't deprived of the standard of life to which she was accustomed. He had no doubt that she'd fall in with any plan he cared to suggest. After a few weeks of marriage, she'd be eating out of his hand. ... As he contemplated the future, he could hardly contain his excitement. ...

At ten o'clock that morning he collected his car from the local garage, where it had been in for a service, and took a quick run into Lingford to see Susan. She and her mother were going up to town for a day or two to pay some calls and do some shopping—and though the parting would be brief, the note of absolute devotion had to be maintained. After he'd seen them off he lunched enjoyably in Newmarket before returning to the site. It was about half past two when he got back. Having nothing better to do, he strolled along the lode to do a little more work on the last of the boat arrivals. It was a smart little cruiser called *Flavia*, brought in the previous day by an owner who had suddenly been called abroad. It had been left in full commission and Hunt had been entrusted with the job of laying it up. He stood on the bank for a moment, admiring its lines. One day, he intended to have a motor yacht of his own. But with luck, he'd be keeping his at Cannes or Monte Carlo. Wine, women and yachts—how was that for a prospect. ...?

He was about to step aboard and continue with the clearing up when he noticed someone approaching the office. A girl in a white coat and a blue-flowered head scarf, carrying a suitcase. He walked back to see what she wanted. As he drew nearer, he had the feeling that he'd seen her somewhere before. Then, suddenly and incredulously, he recognised her.

It was the girl he'd met on holiday ... Gwenda Nicholls. ...

Chapter Three

"Hallo, Alan," Gwenda said.

For a moment, he could find no words. His mind ran quickly back over their last meeting—his unfulfilled promise to write—the false address he'd given her. . . . How the hell had she got on to him? What was he going to say to her. . . .? He didn't know. All he knew was that he was in for a damned sticky encounter—and that it could hardly have come at a worse time. . . .

Take it easy, he told himself. Feel your way. . . .

"Why, hallo," he said.

"You didn't expect to see me again, did you?" Her tone was flat, her face unsmiling, her eyes cold. An icy beauty. . . .

Bitter, he thought. Naturally. Bitter because he'd ditched her. A woman scorned. Probably all set for trouble. And what trouble she could make! He'd have to handle her gently. Soothe her, if he could. Mollify her. . . . But how. . . .?

Admit everything, and pretend to be remorseful. . . .? No, he'd never get away with that—not after what he'd done. . . . Try to bluff his way through? Lie about everything? Then, if the bluff worked, say his feelings had changed and ease her out. . . .? That was more like it. More his line of country. . . .

With a faintly injured air, he said, "I *hoped* to see you."

"What—after giving me the wrong address?"

He looked puzzled, "The wrong address? What do you mean?"

"You know you gave me an address in Brighton."

"*Brighton.* . . .?" He stared at her. "But that's where I'd just moved from. . . ." Suddenly he clapped his hand to his forehead. "Oh, what a damn' fool. . . . ! Gwenda, I must have scribbled down the old one without thinking—I suppose I was so used to it. . . . What a clot!"

A little colour crept into Gwenda's face, a little hope into her eyes. "Is that true?"

"Of course it's true—you don't imagine I'd have given you a wrong one on purpose. . . . Anyway, this was the address I put on my letter. . . ."

"What letter?"

"Why, the letter I wrote to you at Peterborough."

"I never got any letter."

"Surely. . . . ! I wrote to you soon after I got back. Sent it to 19 Everton Road—that's right, isn't it. . . .? I remember posting it in the village box."

"I never got it."

"Then it must be the damned G.P.O. I *wondered* why you never answered. . . . Oh, lord, what a run of bad luck!"

"It's awful," she said. She was searching his face—uncertain, he could see, whether to believe his story—but desperately wanting to. The ice had begun to thaw. Things should go better now.

"Anyway," he said, "if you didn't get my letter, how did you find me?"

"I'd seen your proper address, I saw it on your luggage, the day you left the hotel. On the quay, while you were paying your bill."

"I *see* . . ." Silently, Hunt cursed his carelessness.

"I thought—I thought you'd just been amusing yourself with me. That you didn't mean us to meet again. . . ."

"Was that why you weren't there when the launch left?"

Gwenda nodded. "I was so hurt—so ashamed. . . ."

"You poor kid. . . . I couldn't think what could have happened—I said so in my letter . . . But you really ought to have checked, you know. After all, *that* address could have been an old one—and the one I gave you the right one. Luggage labels are often out of date."

"I know—I thought of that when I got home. I wondered how I could make sure. I was going to write to Brighton and see if anyone answered. . . . Then I thought it would be quicker to telephone the local post office and ask if you lived here—and they said you did. That seemed to settle it. . . . I wouldn't have bothered you again—nothing would have made me. . . . Except what's happened. . . . Alan, I'm going to have a baby."

Hunt's jaw dropped. "*No . . . !*"

"I am."

"Are you sure?"

"Quite sure."

"Oh, my God. . . . !"

Suddenly, the place where they were standing seemed to Hunt altogether too exposed. "Look, let's go and talk in my caravan," he said. He picked up her suitcase and led the way to the van.

Gwenda took off her head scarf and coat and sank gratefully on to the cushioned settee. Hunt gazed at her now with something close to hatred. Pregnant and the very first time! What sort of a deal was that to hand out to a fellow? Just what you'd expect of a Baptist's daughter! It no longer interested him that she was one of the prettiest redheads he'd come across, that if anything she looked more of a tasty dish than ever. He'd had her, and he no longer wanted her. Or anything to do with her. His sole objective now was marriage, wealth and freedom. What a bloody fool he'd been. . . .

"I need a drink," he said. "What about you?"

"No, thanks. . . . I wouldn't mind a glass of milk if you've got some, though."

He poured the milk for her, and a stiff whisky for himself. When he'd downed it, he felt a bit better. This situation was going to take some handling, but he'd manage it somehow. He'd got to . . . First, the crucial question. . . .

"Have you told your parents?"

Gwenda shook her head.

"Have you told anyone?"

"No."

He gave a grunt of relief. "Well," he said, in a friendlier tone, "this is a bit of bad luck—but there's no need to worry . . . I'm sure we can organise something."

"What do you mean?"

"I'll find someone who'll get rid of it for you—it's not hard if you know the right people. . . . I'll lay on all the transport that's needed, and help you work out a story—and of course I'll foot the bill, it won't cost you a penny."

"I don't want to get rid of it," Gwenda said.

Hunt gave a tolerant smile. "Oh, come now, that's just silly."

"*I* don't think it's silly," Gwenda said. "I shouldn't have done what I did in the first place—but I did, and I'm not going to get out of it that way. I don't think it's right."

"Not right . . .? Good heavens, girls do it all the time."

"I don't care—*I'm* not going to . . . I've made up my mind, Alan . . . If that's all you've got to suggest, you can save your breath."

"But Gwenda, be reasonable. . . . What will you *do*?"

There was a little pause. Then she said, "Some people get married. . . . Why shouldn't we?"

He'd been expecting that. For a moment, he didn't answer. What should he tell her? The brutal truth? Half the truth. . . .?

"I wasn't going to suggest it," Gwenda went on, "not when I came. I just thought I ought to tell you about the baby, that's all. . . . I didn't really want anything more to do with you—it seemed so mean, the way you'd gone on. . . . But you've explained things, and I can see now how wrong and unfair I was, and I'm sorry. . . . Now everything's different. . . . After all, we did like each other, didn't we?"

"Of course we did," Hunt said. "And I hope we still do . . . But, Gwenda, things aren't the same any more. I can't marry you now . . . The fact is, I—I've got involved with another girl."

She looked at him disbelievingly. "Oh, Alan . . . ! So soon?"

"Well," he said, "I thought you'd written me off. . . . First you weren't at the quay when the launch left, which shook me, and then you didn't reply to my letter . . . . I thought you must have changed your mind about me—decided I was too old for you, or something . . . I was pretty fed up, actually . . . Then I happened to meet Lesley."

"Who is she?"

"She's the daughter of the man who owns this place. My boss. . . . He happened to bring her along one day, and we got friendly."

"Are you going to marry *her*?"

"Well, we're not officially engaged, but there's a sort of understanding . . . I don't see how I can duck out of it."

"You mean you don't want to?"

"I didn't say that."

"Are you very fond of her?"

"I am quite fond of her, of course. . . . And I am more or less committed."

"You're not as committed as I am," Gwenda said bitterly.

"Well, no . . . Gwenda, I wish I *could* marry you, honestly I do—but I just don't see how I can. . . . Look, be sensible—let me find someone who'll fix it."

"No," Gwenda said. "*No!*" She reached for her suitcase. "I think I might as well be on my way."

"Where are you going to?"

"St. Neots," she said. "I've taken a job there."

"A job . . .? What job?"

"It's with a family called Baker—looking after their little boy."

"So you've finally got away from home?"

"Yes, for the moment. . . . I had to—it was the only way I could come and see you without anyone knowing. . . . I answered the advertisement, and practically settled that I'd go, and then I badgered Mum and Dad till they agreed."

"But you won't be able to keep this job, surely? Now you're pregnant, I mean?"

"I don't have to. It's a temporary job—just for six weeks."

"I see . . . And then what?"

Gwenda sighed. "Then I'll have to go back home and confess, I suppose. . . . What else can I do?"

Hunt sat in appalled silence, staring at her . . . If she told her parents, they'd insist on knowing who the father was. She'd tell them that, too—she owed him no loyalty. They'd find out he was a bachelor, and they'd say he ought to marry her. She'd tell them about the other girl. Then that tin chapel father of hers would come chasing after him. He'd make a hell of a fuss. He'd find out who the other girl really was. Probably he'd go and see Ainger. . . .

And there'd be no marriage to Susan. It was as predictable as nightfall.

A wave of anger swept through Hunt. If this girl talked, he'd be right back where he'd started. All his patient work gone for nothing. All his glittering prospects dashed . . . And why? Because of her idiotic prejudices. . . . Obstinate little bitch! Why the devil couldn't she get rid of the kid, like anyone else would. . . .?

He went over to the caravan window and stood there, gazing across the fen, trying to think of some way out. If she'd been a common tart, he could have bribed her—but she wasn't. If she'd been older, more worldly, he could have offered to set her up in her own establishment and go on providing for her as long as she kept quiet. But she wasn't that, either. She was just a simple, ordinary girl in trouble—and in spite of her earlier talk of independence, he hadn't a doubt that when the crunch came she *would* go back to Mum and Dad. . . . And there was no way he could stop her.

At least. . . .

There *was* a way, of course. . . . If he could bring himself to take it. If he had the guts . . . Or there *might* be . . . It would be a desperate step—as well as a most unpleasant one. But the situation was desperate, too. . . .

No harm, anyway, in seeing how the land lay. . . .

He half turned. Gwenda had made no further move to leave. She was sitting quietly on the settee, watching him. . . . Hoping, no doubt, that he might still change his mind about her.

"Does anyone at all know about you and me?" he asked. "About our having met?"

She shook her head.

"Did you tell anyone you were coming here?"

"No . . . Why . . .?"

"I was just thinking . . ."

That seemed all right—as long as she was telling the truth. Hunt lied so much himself, he was always ready to suspect a lie from others. But she'd answered with an air of truth. . . . Then another possibility occurred to him.

"Did you have any difficulty in finding your way here?"

35

"Not really," she said.

"Surely you had to ask someone?"

"I asked the bus conductor if he knew the place—and a man in the village, when I got off. . . . Then I saw the sign at the end of the drive."

"I see. . . ." So people *did* know she'd come—and they might remember later. Probably they would. Even with that head scarf over her hair, she wasn't a girl men would easily forget. There was that telephone call she'd made to the village post office, too—asking about him. That might be remembered. One way or another, a link with him would almost certainly be established once inquiries began. That meant he'd have to be ready with some story . . . Well, it wouldn't be the first story he'd invented. Already, he had the germ of an idea. . . .

What about the grim undertaking itself? He turned again to the window. The fen had a practical interest for him now. . . . He could see one or two people walking there. It would be hopeless to think of anything in daylight. Sometimes people went there at night, too—but usually they were too busy with each other to notice anyone else. And the reeds were high, completely obscuring the view between one part of the fen and another. If he could think of a way of keeping Gwenda here till nightfall, the chances were that no one would see him. A couple of hours' work, and his troubles could be over. . . .

But dare he risk it? There were other hazards, besides the chance of being seen. Or heard. He could make a mistake—overlook something . . . The way he'd overlooked that luggage label. . . . No one thought of everything . . . There'd be risks in making preparations, risks in covering all traces. The least carelessness could lead to a search—and the body might be found. There would in any case be endless questions—and one slip-up could finish him . . .

Yet one thing was sure—if he didn't do it, he was sunk. It was a clear choice—risk against riches. Wasn't the gamble worth it? And after all he didn't have to decide now. He'd have hours to think about it—to work out a plan. . . . All he had to do *now* was get Gwenda to stick around. If, later in the evening, the dangers seemed too great, he could scrub the whole thing. . . .

Her voice broke in on him. "What are you thinking about, Alan?"

"You," he said. "You and me—and what we're going to do . . ." For a little while longer, he stood debating. . . . If he did get her to stick around, in the only way possible, and then decided to do nothing, he'd have a pretty trying emotional set-up on his hands. But that would be the least of his troubles. . . . Suddenly, as though he'd come to a great decision, he went over to Gwenda and sat down close beside her. His face had softened, his whole manner had changed.

"You know," he said, "I think we ought to marry. I think we'd regret it all our lives if we didn't. I know I should . . . I always meant to ask you to marry me when we got home, anyway. I really did fall for you in Norway. When I didn't hear from you I was terribly miserable. I suppose that's really how I came to get involved with Lesley—a sort of rebound. . . . But I realise now, I can't let you go. It's you I love"

Tears gathered in Gwenda's eyes. "Oh, Alan. . . ."

"What about you, darling? How do you feel?"

"I love you, too, Alan. . . . I think I have ever since I met you. I want to marry you . . . Oh, I've been so unhappy."

He stroked her hair, comforted her. "Well, it's all over now, sweetie. We'll definitely get married. It's settled."

"How about—Lesley?"

"I'll have to tell her I made a mistake, that's all. She's bound to be hurt, I'm afraid—but there's nothing else to be done, is there?"

"No . . ."

"She'll get over it, I'm sure. It's not as though the thing went very deep—not like with you and me. . . . I mean, I never slept with her or anything like that. We were really just good friends. . . ."

"I see. Well, I'm glad about that. . . . When will you tell her?"

"As soon as I can—but she's on a cruise at the moment, she won't be back for a few days. It's just as well, really, because I'm bound to lose this job when her father knows and it'll give me time to look for another one. ... As soon as I've got things straightened out, we'll tell your people, eh? Face the music—get it over."

"Oh, *yes*."

"You'll see, darling—they won't be too angry when they know we're going to get married right away. ... Incidentally, I don't see much point in your going to the Bakers now. Not if we're going to marry in a week or two."

"I've got to go somewhere," she said.

"You can stay here." He smiled at her. "After all, I can't compromise you any more than I have done, can I? And now that I've got you back, I can't bear to let you go again. We've so much to talk about—so many plans to make. ... Do stay—*please* ... You can cook the meals—start getting your hand in. ... It'll be fun."

"I'd love to," she said. "But what about the Bakers?—they're expecting me."

"When?"

"To-night ... Any time after seven, they said. They're going to be out till then."

"Are they on the phone?"

"Yes."

"Then you can ring them up later on—say you're sorry, but you've changed your mind."

"Won't I be letting them down?"

"They'd probably sooner know now—rather than have you go along and then leave in a few days. That would mean a double upset."

"M'm—I expect you're right."

"Good—then everything's settled." Hunt took her in his arms and kissed her tenderly. "Nothing more to worry about at all, eh ...? I'll get another job, we'll look for somewhere to live, we'll make our peace with Mum and Dad, we'll get married, and we'll have our family. Just like any other young couple. It's going to be marvellous. ..."

"Oh, yes. ..." Gwenda's eyes were bright with love and hope.

"There's just one thing," Hunt said. "I think it might be wiser if you didn't show yourself outside too much in daylight. You're pretty eye-catching—and we don't want people talking till I've got that job lined up."

"No—all right."

"Now what about some grub. . . .? A real cosy domestic meal, eh. . . .? And after dark, we'll go for a stroll in the fen. You'll love it—it's very romantic at night. . . ."

He showed her where the food was kept, and how to work the stove. Then he went back to the window. As he'd foreseen, she'd been putty in his hands. A pregnant girl, in love—of course she'd wanted to stay with him. . . . All he had to do now was work out a plan—a good plan. . . . He began to turn over the problems. Problems of timing, of moonlight, of method, of tools, of the best place to choose. Technical problems, that he felt well able to cope with. . . .

It was later on in the evening that anxiety returned. The plan was taking shape nicely—but he was still worried in case he might overlook something.

As things turned out, he was right to be.

PART TWO

Chapter One

It was the receipt of an anonymous letter through the post that caused the police to look into the happenings at Ocken Fen that week-end. The communication, in the form of a letter card, arrived at the brick villa of Police-Constable Blake in Ocken village on the Monday morning. It was addressed in pencilled capital letters to "The Police, Ocken, Cambridgeshire." As he was the only policeman in Ocken, P.C. Blake opened it. The contents were startling, and he reported them at once to his county headquarters. He was instructed to get on his motor-bike and take the letter without delay to Cambridge. There it came, in the first place, into the hands of Sergeant Tom Dyson of the county C.I.D.

Dyson, to look at, was an impressive young officer. He had a splendid physique, dark good looks, alert grey eyes and a strong jaw line. His career had been impressive, too. On the beat he had been efficient and courageous, gaining a merit award on one occasion for tackling a man armed with a gun. In the plain-clothes branch he had shown outstanding qualities. Some detective-sergeants are born to be good plumbers' mates, work-horses for their inspectors. Dyson wasn't one of these. He had an independent and original mind, as well as a logical one. Great things had been prophesied for him. . . . But now, at twenty-nine, he seemed to have put his future behind him.

The turning point had come twelve months before. He had been living at that time with his pretty young wife Mary and his baby daughter Linda in a small but charming stud-and-plaster cottage—largely renovated by himself—in open country just outside Cambridge. They had been blissfully happy there. Dyson, by blood and upbringing, was a countryman—a native of East Anglia, with a feeling for land and for soil, a liking for flat country and wide skies, a knowledge of plants and birds and trees picked up without effort in his childhood and his youth. Mary had shared his tastes. He had liked nothing better in his off-duty periods than to create an idyllic little garden behind the cottage and potter in it with Mary and the baby. So many of the things he saw in the course of his work were sordid and vicious that his home had seemed like a corner of heaven. He'd meant to keep it that way.

Then Mary, out shopping one day in Cambridge, had been felled by an exuberant motorist who said he sounded his horn before he killed her. Dyson, completely shattered, had sold the cottage and all its contents and gone to live in the town with his mother, who was now looking after two-year-old Linda. The tragedy had left him desolate in his personal life, and almost pathological on the subject of motor cars. It couldn't be helped that so many people in the world were stupid, unimaginative, selfish, reckless, but he saw no reason why such people should be allowed to arm themselves with the lethal weapon of the car. In his black and bitter moods he would ask derisively why the Government didn't ban all private motoring and save countless lives by the issue to every adult citizen of a comparatively harmless alternative toy, like a hand grenade. Taking, as he did, this extreme view about a thing that caused a mere eight thousand deaths and a few hundred thousand injuries each year, he was naturally regarded as an eccentric, warped by his own misfortune.

The tragedy had done more than focus his hatred on the motor car. It had left him restless in his work and indifferent to his prospects. For the moment, at least, he had no objective, nothing to strive for. It was no longer clear that he even wanted to be a policeman. Though he still did a competent job, he had lost his zest and purpose. Sometimes he behaved like a man who might any day take a boat to the other side of the world. . . .

The text of the anonymous letter—pencilled, like the address, in block letters—read:

Dear Sir,

Yesterday evening I was up in the old hide on Ocken Fen and about half past eight I saw a man and a girl walking along one of the drives in the moonlight. I watched them disappear round a bend and then I heard the girl give a sort of squeal. I thought they were just larking about and didn't pay any more attention at the time but later on I saw a torch flashing and I watched and presently the man went back along the drove by himself. I don't know who the girl was but I thought the man looked a bit like the one who runs the Cosy Caravan site. Anyway, that was the direction he went off in. I dare say nothing happened, but it's been on my mind and I thought I ought to tell you. I'm sorry I can't give my name but I was with a friend myself and she might get into trouble.

Dyson read the letter through twice, his face registering distaste. He disliked anonymous letters, from every point of view. They were suspect evidence, they rarely gave enough information, and you couldn't question the writers. They were often sent in malice, and quite often by nut cases. Like that poison pen writer he'd helped track down a couple of years before, who'd accused herself of sexual offences. ... Still, this fellow sounded sane enough. ... Dyson looked at the postmark. The stamp had been cancelled at Ocken on Sunday afternoon. The text of the letter was headed "Sunday morning." So the incident, if it had happened, had been on Saturday evening. . . . He glanced in his diary, checking the time of moonrise. Yes, that was all right. . . . Then he heard Chief Inspector Nield enter the office next door, and he took the letter in.

John Nield was a solidly built man in his early fifties, tending to portliness, with a balding head and grizzled brows and moustache. He lived with his wife in a small, detached house on the outskirts of Cambridge. Mrs. Nield was comfortable and domestic, an excellent cook, a natural home-maker, and the mother of a son and daughter who were now both married. She had spent much of her life keeping meals hot, postponing appointments, cancelling holiday arrangements, and generally adapting herself to the irregularities of a policeman's lot. She had often complained, but she had never had any regrets. It had been an interesting and varied life, concerned with human beings and not with things, constantly giving her something new to discuss and share with the husband she was devoted to. At fifty-three, she counted herself a fulfilled and lucky woman.

Though Nield's life had been hard and tough, his features had taken on over the years a remarkably benign expression, so that he looked like somebody's slightly quizzical grandfather. By nature he was an equable and philosophical man. He didn't believe, as some of his colleagues did, that the human race had grown suddenly worse in recent years—or that it was ever likely to grow much better. He knew that the battle against crime would never be wholly won—or wholly lost. You just had to keep on bashing away. Nield himself had bashed, not unsuccessfully, for more than thirty years. His small triumphs had been gained by dogged effort. He had a craftsman's pride in his job, and the tools of his craft were commonsense, humanity and diligence.

His relationship with Sergeant Dyson was friendly and often informal. Nield recognised qualities in the young man that he knew he lacked himself—a flair, an unorthodoxy, an impulsive brilliance on occasion. He was also deeply sorry for him. Nield and his wife had known and liked Mary Dyson, and the tragedy had shocked them. Though Dyson's hurt had been grievous, and these things took time, they both hoped that he would eventually remarry, and find a new purpose, and that the check to his career would be only temporary. He was too good a man, in every way, to be wasted. . . . Dyson, in his turn, had respect for the older man's experience and know-how—though he sometimes felt that Nield had become a little *too* mellow in his judgments. Dyson was inclined to see things as black and white. . . . On the whole, though, they made a good team.

Nield had already been given the gist of the anonymous letter on the telephone. Now, waving Dyson to a chair, he quickly read it through.

"Yes. . . ." he said, after a moment. "Well—what do *you* make of it, Sergeant?"

Dyson shrugged. "Assuming it's on the level, sir, the obvious things . . . It was written by a man with a good deal of local knowledge, so I'd guess he lives around there. An educated man, not a rustic. . . . There'd be plenty of those about, even in a fen village—shopkeepers, farmers, professional people—enough to make tracing impossible, I'd say. . . . Somebody out on the quiet with another man's girl friend or wife, by the sound of it. . . ."

"But otherwise a good citizen, eh? Sense of public duty. . . ."

"He took his time letting us know," Dyson said. "He could have telephoned us on Saturday. . . . For that matter, he could have done a bit of checking up himself."

"Not if he had a woman with him, Sergeant. Not easily. . . ."

"Perhaps not . . . Anyway, I don't think much of his excuse for not giving his name. He could have told us who he was without mentioning the woman at all."

"He'd have known we'd have asked what he was doing in the fen," Nield said. "He might have thought it would be awkward for *him*. Perhaps *he* wasn't supposed to be out—or perhaps he was supposed to be somewhere else. Maybe he was thinking of himself, not the woman."

"That's possible," Dyson agreed.

Nield looked at the letter again. "He's pretty vague about where the incident was supposed to happen."

"Ocken Fen's a pretty vague place, sir. Sort of featureless."

"You know it, do you?"

"I went there for a picnic once—in the old days. . . . It's a very wild spot."

"What's this 'hide' the fellow talks about?"

"I seem to remember there were two wooden towers—look-outs for watching birds. One of them's falling to bits—at least, it was when I was there. I think he must mean that."

"Yes, I see ... Well, it all seems to make pretty good sense. A wooden tower would have been more comfortable for a bit of necking than the damp ground, I suppose. And he'd certainly have had a view from up there. ... What's more, being seen from a tower is the sort of thing anyone planning a bit of mayhem might not have thought of. ... I think we'd better go and see the bloke at the caravan site. Did you get his name?"

"Hunt," Dyson said. "Alan Hunt."

They drove to Ocken in a black police car with a sign above the roof. Dyson was at the wheel. Nield sat back and quietly planned his approach. It would have to be cautious, since they'd almost nothing to go on. The letter writer himself hadn't been sure of his identification. It could well have been some other man in the fen. And there was no real evidence of foul play. The girl could simply have gone off on her own. The whole thing could easily fizzle out. Better, Nield thought, not to produce the letter—not at first, anyway. There was no point in stirring up trouble unnecessarily. A gentle probe—that was the line. ... Preceded, perhaps, by one sharp, testing question. ...

The fen was just over twenty miles from Cambridge—a fifty-minute journey, at Dyson's stately pace. They had their first glimpse of it as they passed the main entrance, where the sergeant pointed out the twin towers of the hides. Then, at a T-junction in the village, Nield spotted the Cosy Caravan sign, and Dyson turned into the drive and pulled up outside the office. They both got out.

After a moment the office door opened and a man emerged. Both detectives watched him closely. He was looking at the car, at the "Police" sign above it. He seemed mildly surprised, nothing more.

"Mr. Alan Hunt?" Nield asked.

"That's right."

"My name is Nield—Chief Inspector Nield. This is Sergeant Dyson. ... I thought you might be able to help us, Mr. Hunt, over a little matter we're looking into. ..."

"Of course—if I can. ..."

"I believe you had a young lady with you on Saturday?"

"A young lady. . . .? Why, yes. . . ." Hunt's face showed sudden concern. "I say, she's not done anything silly, has she?"

"Not as far as I know, sir. . . . I take it she was a friend of yours."

"No, not a friend—she was an acquaintance I met on holiday."

"Would you mind telling me her name?"

"Gwenda Nicholls. . . . What's all this about, Inspector?"

"We've received some information—I'd sooner not go into the details at the moment."

Hunt continued to look puzzled and slightly worried. "Just as you like, of course. . . ."

"Where does this girl live, Mr. Hunt?"

"At Peterborough. . . . 19 Everton Road."

"And she came over here to see you?"

"Well, not exactly. . . . Look, I think it would be much better if you asked *her* about it."

"Now that I'm here, sir, I may as well hear anything you can tell me."

"It's really not my affair," Hunt said uncomfortably. "I don't know that I've the right to talk about her."

"I'm afraid I must insist," Nield said.

"I see . . . Well, that's different . . . I warn you, though, it's a long story."

"We're in no hurry," Nield said, "if you're not."

"In that case, I suggest we go and talk in my caravan. It'll be more comfortable than standing out here."

"Very well," Nield said.

Hunt led the way through the line of vans. Nield walked beside him, exchanging a polite word or two about the nature of the business and the end-of-season quietness. Dyson followed a pace behind, very respectfully. Nield's deft handling of that preliminary interview had struck him as a model. He had no reason, yet, to admire Hunt's handling of it.

"Right, sir," Nield said, when they were all seated. "Let's have your story."

49

"Well," Hunt began, "it was after lunch on Saturday. About three o'clock, I suppose. I was working on a boat at this end of the site when I saw a girl with a suitcase standing at the office door. So I went to see what she wanted. I thought there was something vaguely familiar about her, but I couldn't place her. She looked at me as though she knew me, too—but with a sort of puzzled expression. She asked if Mr. Alan Hunt was around. I said I was Alan Hunt. She looked more puzzled. She said, hadn't we met on holiday in Norway? And then I remembered her. We'd been fellow guests at a hotel for a day or two in August—the Vistasund, near Stavanger. We hadn't had much to do with each other, so you can imagine I was pretty surprised at her showing up here. Anyway, I said I did remember her—and I repeated that I was Alan Hunt. She looked very distressed—said there'd been an awful mistake, and that I wasn't the man she'd expected to see. . . . Then she burst into tears. . . ."

"H'm—quite a drama," Nield said.

"It was most embarrassing, I can tell you. She was really upset—crying and sobbing. I didn't know what to do with her . . . In the end I brought her along here to the van and gave her a drink, and I asked her what was wrong and if I could do anything. At first she didn't want to tell me, she just kept crying, but I coaxed her a bit and suddenly she poured it all out. Apparently she'd been seduced by some man she'd met at the hotel—and she was pregnant. He'd got her tight the night before she'd left—and he'd given her *my* name and address. I suppose he'd seen it on my luggage or something—he must have been a proper shower. Now she'd no idea who or where he was, and she was in a real mess. She'd left home that day to start a new job in St. Neots—she'd taken it specially so she could call in here on the way. This fellow who'd seduced her had said he was a bachelor, and she'd hoped he'd marry her. Now she just didn't know what to do."

"What *did* she do?" Nield asked.

"Well, she began to talk rather wildly—in fact, she got me quite worried. She said she couldn't face it, and that she'd be better off dead. I said that was nonsense—there were thousands of girls who had fatherless babies and most of them got by somehow. Then she said she supposed she'd have to lose herself, hide herself away, and she started talking about changing her name, pretending her husband had died, starting life over again where she wasn't known. It seemed an extraordinary attitude for these days. I said she'd do much better to go back to her parents—and then she told me about them. Apparently they're very strait-laced, and she was scared stiff of them knowing. . . . Well, I talked to her like a Dutch uncle then. I said that whatever her parents were like, they'd look after her, and no one else would, and that however angry they were to start with they'd get over it and probably finish up proud grandparents—all the obvious things. I must have talked for hours, and I had a hell of a job convincing her—but I managed it. In the end, she said she *would* go back and tell them. I gave her a bite to eat, and she rang up the people at St. Neots and said she'd changed her mind about coming to them, and around seven-thirty I drove her back to Peterborough."

"You took her home?"

"Well, I thought I'd better—it's an awkward, cross-country journey, and she'd done it once already that day. Besides, I wanted to make sure she got there. She was a nice girl—I felt really sorry for her . . . And that's about all I can tell you . . . You can see now why I said it was her affair."

Nield nodded . . . For a few seconds there was silence in the caravan. Then the inspector got briskly to his feet. "Well, Mr. Hunt, it sounds to me as though you did a good job in a very trying situation. I congratulate you."

"Thank you," Hunt said.

"And you've certainly helped me with my inquiries."

"I'm glad of that . . . Even though I don't know what they're about!"

Nield smiled. "I'm sorry I can't be more forthcoming."

"Don't worry, Inspector . . . I hope the girl's not got into any more trouble, that's all . . . Give her my regards if you see her."

"I will," Nield said. "Good-bye, Mr. Hunt—and thank you."

"Well, that was a rum story," Dyson said, as they drove away.

"It was," Nield agreed. "So rum that I can't see him making it up. I think our letter writer must have been imagining things."

Dyson grunted. "I noticed he didn't ask us how we got on to him. Bit odd, don't you think?"

"Well, he wasn't exactly encouraged to ask questions, was he . . .? I'd say he's on the level . . . He certainly wasn't at all scared when he saw the car, and he couldn't have been more straightforward about the girl. . . . Did he strike you as a man who'd just got rid of someone in the fen?"

"No, sir, he didn't. . . ."

"Anyway," Nield said, "if the girl's at home, that's the end of it . . . Better head for Peterborough, Sergeant."

Chapter Two

They reached Everton Road shortly before one o'clock. It was a new road on the southern outskirts of the city—part of an estate of superior semis, a black-coated area. Number 19 was the last house but one before a corner. It had the usual neat front garden, with a paved drive leading to a garage.

Nield rang the bell. He could hear voices inside the house, and after a moment a white-haired, pleasant-faced woman came to the door.

"Mrs. Nicholls?" Nield asked, in his best benign-grandfather manner.

"That's, right."

"I believe you have a daughter . . . Gwenda Nicholls?"

"Yes."

"I rather wanted a word with her. Is she at home, by any chance?"

"No," Mrs. Nicholls said, "She's not living here any more. She's working at St Neots. . . . What's it about?"

Nield's face was suddenly grave. Dyson moved a little nearer the door. Far from coming to an end, the case was evidently about to begin.

"I was given to understand that she came back here on Saturday night," Nield said.

Oh, no . . . Who *are* you?"

"We're police officers . . . I wonder if we might . . ."

She broke in anxiously. "What's happened?"

"Now don't alarm yourself, Mrs. Nicholls—it may turn out to be nothing very much . . . May we come in?"

She stepped back to let them pass. "My husband's at home," she said, "you'd better see him . . ." She showed them through the little hall into an empty sitting-room, very clean and neat. A strong smell of friar's balsam hung in the air. "He's been a bit poorly . . ." She went off to fetch him.

Nield and Dyson exchanged bleak glances. "Who'd be a policeman?" Nield said. He braced himself for the inevitable ordeal. Dyson studied the title on a well-filled bookshelf. *Rating and Valuation, The History of Local Government, Livingstone the Pathfinder, The Temperance Movement in the 19th Century, Sermons. . . .*

Mrs. Nicholls was back almost at once with her husband. A grey, spare, austere-looking man, Dyson noted, matching the book titles. Nicholls gave the policeman a brief nod. "What's this about our daughter . . .? What's happened?"

It was a question that Nield couldn't answer—not with certainty. But what he did know—or a part of it—he would now have to tell. The parents had a right to hear it—and must hear it. On the very best interpretation, their daughter was "missing" . . . But he would spare them all he could.

He told them, broadly, what Hunt had told him—making it plain that everything came from Hunt, that he himself took no responsibility for the story. He didn't mention the anonymous letter—that could wait at least till he'd seen Hunt again. One heavy blow at a time was enough.

To Dyson, listening and watching, there was a horrible familiarity about the interview. The homely faces, suddenly strained and grey. The shock, the incredulity, the indignation . . . He'd seen it all before, so many times. . . . Of course Johnny wouldn't have carried a knife—not *Johnny* . . . Of course Jane wouldn't have stolen from the shop—not *Jane* . . . Trusting parents, trusting spouses, full of faith and empty of knowledge . . . And now these two . . . Gwenda made drunk by a strange man—impossible! Gwenda seduced—unthinkable! Gwenda pregnant—unbelievable! Gwenda going off to St. Neots so deceitfully, afraid to tell her own parents the truth—she'd never have done that. . . .

Then, with tears flowing and anxiety rising, the painful adjustment to the facts. Well, yes—looking back now, Mrs. Nicholls *could* see that Gwenda might have been pregnant. She hadn't been well one morning. She'd been so unhappy, too, the last few days. She'd been quite desperate to get away ... But how could it have happened—especially at that hotel ...? And she'd always been such a good girl. Watched over so carefully, always guarded from evil ... It was the very last thing anyone would have expected. . . .

After the acceptance, the worry about what could have happened to her. . . . Bewilderment that she'd returned to Peterborough but hadn't come home—that at the last moment she'd apparently changed her mind again. The unspoken fear roused by that phrase "better off dead" . . . . Nicholls's hand going out to his wife's in attempted reassurance. . . .

Yes, it was all familiar—the self-deception and the suffering. But Dyson's sympathy was more than ordinarily aroused. At least these two had dignity. There'd been no outbursts, no hysteria, no anger. They were facing up to unbearable facts with courage. They were doing pretty well. . . .

Now came the police questions. Nield put the hopeful-sounding ones first. Whatever his fears, there was routine ground to cover—and he *might* be wrong.

"Assuming," he said, "that your daughter changed her mind again on the very doorstep, is there anyone you can think of whom she might have gone to. ... Has she any close friends in Peterborough?"

"There's Sally," Mrs. Nicholls said. "Sally Thomas ... She's Gwenda's best friend—they've known each other since they were children ... But Sally lives with her mother, and Gwenda never has stayed with them. I shouldn't think she'd be there."

"No," Nield agreed. "Still, we'll take Sally's address, if you don't mind—we might want to talk to her. . . ."

"It's 13, Alport Street—not very far from here. . . . She works in the Central Library—that's where she'd be now."

Nield nodded. Dyson made a note of the address.

"What about other friends?" Nield asked. "Does Gwenda know anyone who lives alone? Or shares a place with other girls?"

"Oh, no."

"How about relatives? Is there anyone she was particularly close to? Anyone she might have taken into her confidence?"

Mrs. Nicholls shook her head. "I've got a brother in Manchester but we hardly ever see him ... There's no one else, really."

Out of the depressed silence, Nicholls came up with a suggestion. "If she changed her mind about coming here, Inspector, mightn't she have changed her mind again about the Bakers—the family at St Neots ...? And gone to them after all?"

Nield looked at him doubtfully. "She'd have had a job getting back there at that time in the evening. Still, we'd better check ... Are the Bakers on the telephone?"

"Yes—I can give you their number. ... "Nicholls consulted his diary. "St. Neots 85438."

"Have you a telephone here?"

"I'm afraid not ..."

"There's a box just round the corner," Dyson said. "Shall I try them?"

Nield nodded. Dyson went off. Nicholls said, "I think she might just have managed it. And it would have been the obvious thing for her to do." Mrs. Nicholls said, "I know there's a train to Cambridge about nine." They waited, hopefully,

Dyson had no hope at all. But he welcomed the opportunity to confirm the facts they had, and perhaps glean a few more.

He got through to St. Neots without trouble. A man's voice answered.

"Mr. Baker?" Dyson said.

"Yes. ..."

"This is the Cambridge County Police, sir. I understand you engaged a Miss Gwenda Nicholls to come to you last Saturday evening. Could I have a word with her?"

"I'm afraid not," the man said. "She didn't come."

"Oh?—how was that?"

"She rang up and called it off. . . . She was supposed to be coming to look after our small son. It was very annoying, actually."

"Who spoke to her, sir—you or your wife?"

"I did."

"And what exactly did she say?"

"Only that she'd changed her mind and was sorry . . . I asked her what had happened, but she merely repeated that she was sorry, and hung up. She seemed in a great hurry—we only exchanged a few words."

"What time was this call?" Dyson asked.

"Just before half past seven in the evening. . . . Is the girl in trouble, Officer?"

"I'm afraid she may be, "Dyson said. "Anyway, I'm much obliged to you . . . Good-bye, sir—and thank you."

He walked quickly back to the house and reported.

Mrs. Nicholls dabbed her eyes. Nield pressed on with his unpromising routine. "Of course," he said, "we must bear in mind what your daughter said about 'losing' herself . . . She could have gone back to that idea."

"If she did," Nicholls said, "she could be anywhere."

"Well, within limits . . . Do you know how much money she had with her?"

"About ten pounds," Mrs. Nicholls said.

"H'm—she could certainly have gone quite a way with that. Still, wherever she is, she's not out of reach . . . I think you'd better let me have a description of her."

Dyson took down the particulars. . . . Aged twenty, five feet three, chestnut hair worn shoulder length, dark blue eyes. Wearing an off-white woollen coat, a pale blue jumper and pleated grey skirt, a blue-flowered head scarf, navy blue shoes. Carrying a navy blue handbag and a small white suitcase. Initials G.L.N. printed in black letters close to the handle, and a green label of the Vistasund Hotel still stuck on the side . . .

"Have you a photograph of her?" Nield asked.

"Yes—we had one done last Christmas. I'll get it. . . ." Nicholls left the room, and returned almost at once with a frame. He took the photograph out and gave it to Nield. "You can keep it if you want to—we've got another one. . . ."

Nield studied the picture. "What a pretty girl!" he said. He passed it to Dyson. The sergeant sat staring at it, his face grim. The girl in the photograph wasn't just pretty. He was seeing her in colour, as her mother described her, with the long chestnut hair and the deep blue eyes. She must have been beautiful. The dimpled smile was charming, the expression vivacious. . . . A face full of hope and promise. Promise, Dyson feared, that would never now be fulfilled. Such a waste . . . The Nichollses' misery seemed to echo his own loss. . . .

The sergeant had been waiting for an opportunity to ask a few questions himself. There was a point that seemed to him to have great bearing on the next stage of the inquiry—and one that so far had only been touched on. . . . The nature of the relationship between Gwenda and her parents. Had Hunt accurately reported it . . .? Now, with an acquiescent nod from Nield, he put his questions bluntly to both of them.

"If your daughter had come to you," he said, "and told you that she was going to have a baby, what would your attitude to her have been?"

Mrs. Nicholls looked at her husband. "Well—we'd have been deeply shocked—of course . . . Mr. Nicholls and I have strong principles about that sort of thing . . . We'd have been very upset indeed."

"I can understand that," Dyson said. "But what would you have done? Would you have rejected her? Would you have turned her out?"

"Turned her out!" Nicholls said. "Good gracious, no. . . . She's our daughter, after all. . . . We'd have been shocked, as Mrs. Nicholls has said. There'd have been some very straight talking. . . . But we're none of us free from sin, and sin has to be forgiven—as we hope for forgiveness ourselves. . . ."

"So you'd have helped her?" Dyson said.

"Naturally we'd have helped her. We'd have done, I suppose, what other parents do when they find themselves in this dreadful situation. We'd have tried to get her married to the man, if it was possible. . . . If not, we'd have looked after her."

"Surely your daughter knew you well enough to realise this?"

"I would have thought so . . . We've been stern with her sometimes, I'll admit, but never unkind."

"Yet she seems to have been so afraid of you that she didn't dare to face you."

"I don't understand that," Nicholls said. "We've had our ups and downs with her, our disagreements and arguments—but I can't believe she was ever frightened of us . . . Most of the time we all got on very well together."

"Did you part on friendly terms?"

"Yes, indeed . . . Her mother and I hadn't wanted her to leave home yet—we'd often had words about that—but last week she worked herself into such a state that in the end we gave our permission. And once we'd done that, we did everything we could for her. Mrs. Nicholls helped her with her clothes and I looked up the trains and saw her off, and she was going to write . . . We parted on the best of terms, I would have said."

"M'm. . . . Well, in the light of all this, Mr. Nicholls, your daughter's talk of going off and 'losing' herself does seem surprisingly extreme."

"It's unbelievable. . . . I can't imagine what could have come over her."

"And that other talk of hers—about not being able to face life, about being better off dead. . . . That sounds even more extreme."

"Unless she was seriously ill in her mind," Nicholls said solemnly, "I'm sure she would never have thought of harming herself—not for a moment. . . . Apart from anything else, she'd have known it wouldn't be right."

Dyson looked at Nield. "That's all from me, sir. . . ."

The inspector gave him a little nod of approval.

Nield turned finally to the questions he'd had most in his mind all the time. "Before we go," he said, "I'd like to ask you something about your stay at the hotel in Norway ... Can you remember if there was any man your daughter seemed specially friendly with?"

"There wasn't," Mrs. Nicholls said emphatically. "That's what makes it so extraordinary ... Most of the time, the three of us were on our own together."

"In the evenings, too?"

"Well, naturally, we talked to people in the evenings—it was like a big party then. And Gwenda had a dance or two ... But she always came back to sit with us—she didn't go off on her own. I can't see how she could possibly have got to know anyone."

"Of course," Nield said, "the young do have a way of getting together sometimes without their elders knowing ... I assume she had a room of her own in the hotel?"

"Well, yes ..."

There was a little pause. Then Nield said, "By the way, do you remember anything of this Alan Hunt that your daughter saw on Saturday?"

"I seem to remember the name," Mrs. Nicholls said. "That's all. ..."

"He's a tall man, well set-up, very good-looking. About thirty. Fair curly hair and a rather fetching grin."

"Oh, yes—I do remember him now. He was one of the men Gwenda danced with."

"Did she dance with him often?"

"No—only once or twice."

"He didn't become friendly with you as a family—join you in outings—that sort of thing?"

"Oh, no—we hardly knew him. We only saw him at meals, and in the evenings."

"Do you remember when he left?"

"*I* do," Nicholls said. "It was a day or two. before we did ... I remember seeing him in the launch, the morning he went off."

"Was your daughter there, do you recall?"

"I don't think she was . . ." Nicholls looked hard at Nield. "Inspector, are you suggesting. . . ."

"No, Mr. Nicholls," Nield said firmly. "I'm just covering the grounds—that's all. . . ."

He got to his feet. "Well, I think that's as far as we can go at the moment. . . . We'll do our very best to locate your daughter—and of course if we get any news, we'll let you know at once. If you hear anything, please get in touch with me at Cambridge." He gave Nicholls his card. "Good-bye, Mrs. Nicholls. Good-bye, sir. . . ."

Dyson slipped the car into gear. Nield said, "Let's go and have a word with Sally Thomas while we're here."

They found her at the "returned books" desk of the library—a thin, very plain girl, with glasses. Just the sort of friend, Nield couldn't help thinking, that Gwenda's parents would have approved of. No risk of *her* leading anyone into mischief. . . . He introduced himself, and took her aside. The interview was brief, and the result a total blank . . . No, Sally said, she hadn't seen Gwenda since the previous Thursday, when she'd been told about the St. Neots job. No, Gwenda hadn't said anything to her about going to see a man on the way. No, she hadn't ever mentioned meeting a man on holiday. . . . What had happened, Sally asked anxiously. She looked very distressed when Nield told her that Gwenda hadn't gone to St. Neots after all, and that he wasn't quite sure where she was at the moment. "No doubt she'll turn up," he said, with a forced smile. He was hating his job to-day. But what could he do. . . .?

He re-joined Dyson, and briefly reported. "Right, Sergeant—we'll get a bite to eat now. . . . Then back to see Hunt."

"I can hardly wait," Dyson said.

Chapter Three

That second visit of the police to Ocken began inauspiciously for Hunt.

As Dyson drove slowly into the village, a cream sports car flashed across the bows of a lorry at the T-junction, swerved and braked in a skilful avoiding action, and shot away into the Cosy Caravan site.

"I believe that was our man," Nield said.

Dyson's eyes narrowed. "They drive as they live." His tone was bitter.

The inspector gave a non-committal grunt.

Hunt was just getting out of his car as the policemen drove up to the office. "Hallo, Inspector," he called. "Just a second. . . ." He walked to the front of the car and glanced nonchalantly at a tyre. Then he strolled over and joined them. "Two visits in one day, eh? You'll be getting me a bad name."

"We've just come from Peterborough," Nield said.

"Ah, yes. . . . Has the erring daughter made her peace with Mum and Dad?"

Nield shook his head. "She's not there, Mr. Hunt. . . . She didn't go home on Saturday."

"Didn't go home. . . . !" Hunt stared at him. "But that's not possible. . . . Why, I practically saw her to the door."

"But not quite?"

"Well, no. . . ."

"A pity," Nield said. "Was there any particular reason why you didn't?"

"Only that she was giving the directions—and she asked me to stop before we got there. She said, 'This'll do—our house is just round the corner,' or words to that effect—so I pulled up. I thought she probably didn't want to be seen getting out of a jazzy sports car."

"So what happened?"

"She thanked me for bringing her, and I wished her luck, and she went off round the corner."

"I see. . . . Well, she definitely didn't go home."

"Extraordinary!" Hunt said. He stood frowning. "And you've no idea where she did go?"

"No"

"Well, I'm damned . . . ! And I thought I'd done such a good job on her. . . . I suppose she must have got cold feet at the last moment and gone off—the way she'd talked of doing. It looks as though I wasted my day."

"Did she show any signs of having second thoughts while she was in the car?"

"She didn't *say* anything. . . . But she did seem to be getting more and more gloomy the farther we went. I thought it was just because the moment of confession was getting near. Now I can see—she must have been changing her mind."

"H'm. . . . Well, your explanation may be the right one."

"Could there be any other, Inspector?"

"There could be," Nield said. He looked hard at Hunt. "It could be that Gwenda Nicholls has been murdered."

He watched tensely for any change of expression that might be interpreted as a sign of guilt. All he saw was consternation.

"*Murdered*. . . . ! Good God, what makes you say that?"

"We received an anonymous letter this morning, Mr. Hunt. . . . I've no idea who wrote it or how far it can be relied on. Usually I don't pay too much attention to unsigned letters—but this is one I can't ignore. . . . It concerns you—you'd better read it."

Hunt took the letter card and read it through. A look of incredulity spread slowly across his face.

"Are you suggesting, Inspector, that the girl mentioned here was Gwenda Nicholls. . . .? And that I killed her?"

"No," Nield said. "I'm simply looking into the possibility. . . . With that letter before me, and knowing that a girl who was with you here on Saturday has disappeared, I've no alternative."

"But it's the most ridiculous thing I ever heard in my life . . . This fellow's completely up the pole—I never went near the fen on Saturday . . . And by eight-thirty I was nearly at Peterborough—and Gwenda Nicholls was with me. I told you."

"I know you did, sir. . . . But can you prove it?"

"*Prove* it . . . ?" Hunt looked uncertainly at Nield. "That's asking something, Inspector . . . How can I?"

"Did you buy any petrol on the way? Did you stop anywhere? Did you talk to anyone?"

"No—I drove straight there."

"Well, you'd better tell me all you can about the journey. . . . I think you said you left here about half past seven?"

"About that—I didn't notice the exact time . . . It was just after Gwenda had rung up the Bakers."

"I see . . . And which way did you go?"

"Through Stretham, St. Ives and Huntingdon—and straight up the Great North Road."

Nield nodded. "That was the route we used . . . How far was it, Sergeant?"

"Forty miles," Dyson said.

"About an hour's run, eh, Mr. Hunt?"

"At his speed," Dyson said.

"That's right," Hunt agreed. "We got there a little after half past eight."

"And you dropped the girl and came straight back?"

"Well, no—I dropped the girl and sat in the car for a few minutes."

"Oh! Why did you do that?"

"I was tired—I'd had a pretty strenuous afternoon . . . I sat and smoked a cigarette before I left."

"That was at a point just short of Everton Road, was it?"

"It was, if Gwenda was telling the truth. . . . I couldn't swear to it myself—I might have been anywhere . . . You've seen the place—it's

64

one of those suburbs where the roads all look alike. And of course it was dark."

"You had to find your way out of the suburb. Didn't you notice any of the street names then?"

"No—I simply reversed the car and came out the way I went in."

"H'm . . . And what time did you get back here?"

"Some time before ten—I don't know exactly. . . . Anyway, Inspector, this is all quite fantastic. . . . Why on earth should I have wanted to kill Gwenda Nicholls? I hardly knew her."

"That's what you tell me, Mr. Hunt—but again I've only your word for it. . . . I don't say your story about someone else giving your name and address isn't credible—but in view of what's happened since, a doubt does creep in . . . Maybe Gwenda Nicholls *did* find the right man?"

Hunt shook his head. "She didn't, you know."

"If she had, of course, you'd have had a motive."

"For killing her? Just because she was pregnant?"

"It's happened," Nield said. "Often"

"Well, it certainly wouldn't have been a motive for me—what a ghastly thought! Anyhow, I can assure you I wasn't the man. It was some fellow who arrived shortly before I left."

"How do you know?"

"Well, we worked it out . . . I knew when I left, and Gwenda knew when he got there. . . . Not that I've any recollection of him myself—chaps were pouring in and out by every launch. . . ."

"Did she describe him to you?"

"She said he was good-looking and attractive—though she practically had to say that, since she'd let him seduce her. She didn't go into any details, and I didn't press her. . . . At that point I guess she just didn't want to talk about him."

"Wasn't she going to make any effort to trace him . . .? Through the hotel, for instance?"

"No—once she knew how he'd cheated her over the address, she didn't want anything more to do with him."

"Did she tell you what happened? How the seduction came about?"

"She told me a little. . . . Apparently she'd been having a last dance with this chap, and her parents had gone up to bed, and she was on the point of going, too, and then he persuaded her to have a drink in the bar. She wasn't used to drinking and she got a bit squiffy. Afterwards he went upstairs with her, and chatted her into letting him go into her room for a moment, and produced a bottle—and the rest followed. She said it would never have happened if she hadn't been fed up with her parents for keeping her on a leash. She could hardly believe it next day."

"I can imagine . . . And you were already on your way home when this took place?"

"I was already back in England. . . . Honestly, Inspector, you're quite wrong if you think I was the man. As I told you, I didn't know her. Apart from a couple of dances, I hardly spoke to her."

"H'm. . . . Were you accompanied on this holiday, Mr. Hunt?"

"No—I was alone."

"You were alone. . . . And yet you hardly spoke to an exceptionally lovely girl—I've seen her photograph, you know—an attractive, unattached girl, whom you'd danced with? You made no attempt to follow up the acquaintance. . . .? That sounds singularly unenterprising."

"An affair was the last thing I was looking for," Hunt said. "I happened to be engaged to be married."

"Ah . . . That could make a difference, I agree. Faithful to the girl you'd left behind, eh . . .?" Nield looked thoughtful. "Of course, it could also have given you a stronger motive. If you *had* seduced Gwenda Nicholls, and she'd arrived here pregnant, and had threatened to tell your fiancée, you'd have had a classic reason for wanting to get rid of her."

"You mix with bad types, Inspector. . . . As far as I'm concerned, that's pure nonsense."

"Who is your fiancée, Mr. Hunt?"

"Her name's Susan Ainger—she lives near Newmarket. She's a hotel receptionist at the Crown there."

"How long have you known her?"

"About six months."

66

"How long have you been engaged to her?"

"Since July."

"And when do you plan to get married?"

"In December."

"M'm. . . . You hav'n't exactly let the grass grow under your feet, have you . . .? How did you come to meet her?"

"Well," Hunt said, "it was just one of those chances . . . She advertised her sports car in one of the motoring journals, and it was a model I was interested in. I was working in Norwich at the time, but I managed to get down here and she took me for a trial run. . . . That's the car—I bought it from her. . . . Anyway, we got on very well together—and I went on seeing her."

"From Norwich?"

"No—I changed my job soon afterwards."

"Where were you before?"

"With Central Motors."

"Why did you change?"

"I wanted to be near Susan."

"I see . . . I was wondering what had brought you to a quiet spot like this."

"Well, that's the answer . . . I'd fallen for her, and it seemed the only way to get to know her."

"Is she attractive?"

"*I* think she is, naturally. . . . She's not what you'd call pretty, but she's very lively and gay. And we've got a lot of interests in common."

"I shall look forward to meeting her," Nield said.

Hunt stared at him. "Do you have to?"

"I think I may."

"You don't mean you're going to tell *her* about your crazy suspicions?" Hunt's air of slightly amused detachment had suddenly changed to alarm.

"*I* shan't tell her," Nield said. "But she'll almost certainly hear about everything from other sources . . . There's bound to be a lot of publicity from now on."

"Publicity. . . ."

"I'm afraid so. A girl's missing, Mr. Hunt If she doesn't show up in the next day or two, I shall have to circulate her description and give her last known whereabouts. This caravan site. . . . I shall need to enlist the help of the newspapers. They'll no doubt send reporters to interview you—and they'll want to know everything. . . ."

"But—good heavens!—this could just about finish me."

"Not if you've told the truth, sir—and if we find Gwenda Nicholls."

"That's all very well—but suppose you don't . . .? If she's changed her name, and deliberately hidden herself away, you may never find her. Then I'll go on being under suspicion. . . . It's pretty damned unfair, Inspector—just because I did what I could for the girl. . . ."

"Not *just* because of that, Mr. Hunt. There's the letter—remember . . .?"

"The letter's a load of rubbish," Hunt said angrily. "I don't know what the fellow saw, or thinks he saw, but he certainly didn't see me."

"What's your explanation of the incident?"

"A couple of locals having a frolic and going home separately, I'd guess."

"What do you suppose made the writer think of you?"

"How would I know . . .? Seeing the chap walk off in this direction, maybe. If he looked anything at all like me, that could have been enough to account for the mistake, in a bad light. . . . Anyway, it *was* a mistake. Damn it, the writer himself admits he isn't sure. . . . How vague can you get?"

Nield grunted. "Well, we'll leave that for the moment, Mr. Hunt. . . . Now, if you've no objection, I'd like to take a look round."

"I object to your whole attitude, Inspector. I've got caught up in something I know nothing about and I bloody well resent it. . . . But go ahead—I can't stop you. There are forty-five caravans, eighteen boats and ten acres of site. . . . I wish you joy."

"I don't plan a search," Nield said, "just a quick once-over . . . And I'd be glad if you'd come along with us."

Hunt gave an angry shrug. "You might as well arrest me and be done with it."

"Don't push your luck," Dyson said.

Chapter Four

Both policemen knew roughly what they were looking for. This was routine. . . . First, any signs of violence around the site. According to the letter, if a murder had taken place it had occurred in the fen—but traces were often carried back by a killer. . . . Second, any indication that Hunt had recently been out on a digging operation. . . . Third, anything that might have been useful to him in the transport line—since he'd have had to do a good deal of fetching and carrying before the job was over. . . . Finally, anything unusual or out of place—anything that couldn't be adequately explained. . . .

They stopped first at the shed. It was a spacious building, with racks and shelves piled with neatly arranged stores in great variety. Most of the stuff was gear and supplies for the boats and their owners—bottled gas and paraffin, cookers and sleeping bags, rope, oars, clothing, fishing tackle, odds and ends. . . . One shelf was stacked with mattresses and cushions brought in for the winter. Near the door there were some used tools—two shovels, a pick and a spade. They'd been roughly cleaned before they'd been put away, but a little earth still clung to them. Dyson tried to dislodge a piece with his finger nail. It was rock hard. No one had dug with these tools for days.

"Have you got any more spades around?" he asked.

Hunt shook his head. "This isn't a cemetery." he said.

Nield's glance fell on a well-worn suit of overalls hanging from a hook. "Are these yours, Mr. Hunt?"

"They are."

Dyson said, "What do you wear them for? Your dirty work?"

"That's right, Sergeant." Hunt ignored the crack.

Nield took the overalls down and examined them. They had several patches of damp mud on them, and a lot of oil marks.

"No bloodstains?" Hunt said.

"None that leap to the eye, Mr. Hunt. . . . What do you do about footwear?"

"I use gumboots," Hunt said, pointing to a pair in the corner. Nield picked them up. Damp black mud clogged the soles, and wet patches showed on the sides.

"When did you last wear this outfit?"

"Yesterday morning."

"Doing what?"

"I'm clearing out a boat that's just come in—laying it up for the winter. . . . The bank's always muddy at this time of year. In fact, the whole place is muddy."

"So I see," Nield said, moving on.

They stopped next by Hunt's mahogany dinghy. It was tied up to a tree, with the oars across the thwarts.

"Is this your boat?" Nield asked.

"It belongs to the firm. . . . I use it."

"What for, exactly?"

"To take heavy supplies to the cruisers—bottled gas, that sort of thing. And to cross to the other side."

Nield gazed at the unbridged lode. "Do you cross often?"

"Only when I feel like a walk," Hunt said.

"How do most people enter the fen?"

"They're supposed to go through the main entrance and sign a book—but the locals often don't bother, they go in any way they can. . . . I've permission to cross here."

Dyson said, "If a man was seen walking back from the fen in this direction, could he be going anywhere except to the site?"

Hunt gave him a nasty look. "Yes, he could, Sergeant. He could be intending to take the path to the entrance that runs along the other side of the lode. Or he could be going to get into a boat that he'd left tied up to the bank, and row away. . . . Any more bright ideas?"

"I will have," Dyson said. To Nield they seemed like a couple of stags, clashing their antlers.

Dyson climbed down into the dinghy and carefully examined it. The floorboards were damp and muddy, and showed footmarks. All had been made by large gumboots. . . . He took the boards up and looked in the bilges. He found nothing of interest. . . .

They moved to Hunt's caravan. Hunt unlocked the door and stood back with studied contempt. "Help yourselves," he said, "I'll wait. . . ."

"Thank you," Nield said gravely.

Inside, the policemen went meticulously over Hunt's wardrobe and effects. They found more traces of mud, on trouser bottoms—but only small, dry specks. Dyson produced a powerful, waterproof torch from a drawer, and a pair of clumsy leather gauntlets, stiff with dried mud.

Nield stood for a moment at the caravan window, gazing out. A thin autumn mist was beginning to settle over the fen, dimming the last of the afternoon sun. In all the vast expanse he could see only a handful of people—a picnicking couple packing up their tea things, a girl student with a notebook watching something in the reeds, a solitary angler. . . . It all looked very peaceful now, he thought. But what had it been like on Saturday night. . . .?

"Well," Hunt said, as they stepped down, "did you find any buttons torn off my clothes?"

Nield shook his head. "That's a fine torch you've got in there."

"Yes. . . . I suppose you find it sinister?"

"I find it consistent. . . . Do you wear any other sort of gloves except those heavy ones?"

"No."

"Let me see your hands."

With a shrug, Hunt held them out. Nield examined the backs. He found nothing but one or two old, healed scars.

They walked slowly on along the lode past the line of cruisers. Most of the boats had tarpaulins over them. Some had pram dinghies roped to their cabin tops. Dyson glanced inside one or two of the cabins as they passed. Nield stopped beside *Flavia*, looking at the churned-up ground. A plank had been laid over the mud, and the cabin door was open. "I take it this is the boat you're working on," he said.

"That's right. . . . You can see how filthy the place is. Even with the plank, the mud splashes."

Dyson took a step or two along the plank.

"That's right, Sergeant," Hunt said, "you go and have a look. . . . That's where the clues are!"

Dyson poked his head inside the disordered cabin, glanced around, and returned to the bunk.

"You could take a sample of the mud," Hunt said. "Check it with what's on my boots. Have them both analysed."

Nield said, "Where do you burn your rubbish, Mr. Hunt?"

"There's an incinerator behind the shed."

They walked over to it. Nield removed the lid, felt the ashes. They were cold. He poked among the ashes with a stick. There was some partly consumed rubbish, mostly paper. No clothing. . . .

"I hav'n't used it for days," Hunt said.

They came to Hunt's car and casually looked it over. There were the usual tools in the boot, various oddments in the glove box, some groceries and a bunch of bronze chrysanthemums on the passenger seat. Nothing else. . . . Then, as Dyson was about to close the driver's door, a sticker on the door pillar caught his eye. It said, "Serviced, October 3, 1964," and gave the name of the garage. It also gave the car mileage at the time of service—12,143.

Dyson glance at the speedometer. The mileage reading was now 12,305. Just over a hundred and sixty miles since Friday. . . .

Hunt was watching him with cold hostility. "You see, Sergeant—I did go to Peterborough."

"You could have done," Dyson said. "But you could easily have knocked off the miles some other way. . . . Yesterday and to-day."

"Well, I didn't," Hunt said. "Yesterday I did about sixty miles for fun. And all I did to-day was buy some grub and go to a local nursery to get some flowers for Susan. . . ." He gave a bitter laugh. "A fat lot of good flowers are going to do me now. . . . !"

Chapter Five

It had been a good act—that was Dyson's view. A glib liar and a skilful operator had had his answers ready and his tracks well covered. ... Nield was more cautious—he preferred to suspend judgment until he had some solid facts. The best hope of getting any obviously lay in the evidence of the letter and what they might be able to discover in the fen. There wasn't enough daylight left to start work that day—but to-morrow, Nield said, they would come back and take a long, close look at the place.

He was reckoning without the weather. There was enough mist at Cambridge next morning to make him ring up P.C. Blake at Ocken and ask what conditions were like over the fen—and the report was bad.

"Very thick, sir," Blake told him. "It's been thick all night—and you still can't see more than a yard or two. ... They say it'll clear around midday, though."

Nield hung up, frowning. Good visibility was essential for the job they had in front of them. He'd do better to spend the morning catching up on his paper work. Meanwhile, Dyson could be filling a gap in their knowledge.

He called the sergeant in. "I'd like you to take a run over to Newmarket," he said, "and make some discreet inquiries about the Ainger family. Go in your own car, and don't let on that you're the police—I don't want to start any premature rumours. ... Give me a ring around twelve, and if the mist's gone I'll meet you at Ocken."

Dyson nodded. It was the sort of job he welcomed. An inquiry he could, organise in his own way.

Visibility was already beginning to improve by the time he reached Newmarket. He drove first to the Crown Hotel to have a look at Hunt's fiancée. From a passing waiter carrying coffee he was able to discover which of the two young women behind the reception desk was Susan Ainger. He took a seat in the foyer and for some minutes observed and listened. His conclusions were clear-cut and quickly reached. The girl was amiable and jolly; she was well-spoken, well-groomed and very well-dressed. But she was *extremely* plain. It was hard to believe that her charms alone could have been such an irresistible magnet for a man that after a single meeting he'd have thrown up his job and moved a hundred miles in order to be near her. . . . Not that one could ever be sure about those things. . . . But Dyson was already beginning to suspect that there might have been other attractions. Those clothes were expensive. . . .

He went into the phone booth in the foyer and looked up the Aingers in the book. There was only one family of that name living in the immediate neighbourhood—at Lingford. He consulted a road map, and set off. Fifteen minutes and two inquiries later, he reached Copper Beaches. He parked his car on the grass verge a hundred yards beyond it and strolled back to look at the property. There were still patches of mist around, but not enough to obscure the view. And a splendid view it was. . . . He noted the long, agreeable elevation of the house; the pretty cottage and the large paddock; the spacious garage; the well-kept paths and lawns and the stately trees; the blazing beds of dahlias and chrysanthemums and Michaelmas daisies that told of full-time care by experts. A lovely country home. . . . Worth, Dyson thought, at a rough estimate, about thirty thousand pounds. . . .

He drove on into Lingford village, found the local pub, the Horseshoe, and turned into the car park to sit out the ten minutes until opening time. So far, his reconnaissance was going well. He was covering the ground without any fuss—and another piece of the jigsaw was falling neatly into place. . . . All the same, something troubled him. Not just the saddening nature of the case itself—the growing likelihood that Hunt had murdered a charming and lovely girl for the most sordid of ends. Something technical. . . . At the back of his mind, Dyson had a curious feeling that he'd overlooked an important point—that something he'd seen that morning didn't fit. . . . And he knew it would go on nagging at him. . . .

As soon as the pub opened, Dyson went in, ordered a pint of bitter in the saloon bar, and fell into amiable conversation with the landlord. At a suitable moment, he mentioned his supposed business. He was down from London, he said, for a firm of estate agents and was interested in a house, called Copper Beeches.

"We've a well-to-do client," he explained, "who happened to see the house the other day when he was passing, and wants to buy it. He believes that every man has his price, and he wants us to try and talk the owner into selling. . . . But my guess is he's going to be unlucky."

"Yes, I don't reckon you'll get anywhere with Mr. Ainger," the landlord said. "He loves that place—and he's got all the money he needs."

"He has, eh?"

"Good heavens, yes—he's rolling. . . . He's one of these big property chaps. I wouldn't be surprised if he could sit down and write a cheque for half a million."

"Then I'm obviously wasting my time," Dyson said. He paused. "I suppose he's got a family, too—and they probably like the place."

"He's got a wife, and one grown-up daughter. She rides in the paddock there quite a bit."

"M'm. . . ." Dyson sipped his beer. "Not bad being the only daughter of a man with half a million, eh?"

"I'll say. . . . But she's pretty well-heeled without her old man. There's money on her mother's side of the family, too, and she got left ninety thousand quid by her grandmother—came into it on her twenty-first birthday. It was in the local paper—they had a picture of her. Newmarket Heiress, they called her."

"I give up!" Dyson said.

Now he hadn't any doubt at all about Hunt. The picture was complete. . . . A lecher, a fortune-hunter—and a murderer. . . . Well, at least he wouldn't get away with it. . . .

At the first telephone box, Dyson stopped and reported his findings to the inspector.

Nield took the news with outward calm. "Good work, Sergeant. . . . How's the weather there?"

"Clearing fast, sir."

"Right," Nield said. "I'll see you at the main entrance to the fen in an hour from now."

To Nield, also, there no longer seemed much room for doubt. As he drove towards Ocken, he mentally totted up the points against Hunt . . .

The fellow had had as good an opportunity as anyone to seduce Gwenda Nicholls. The story he'd told to account for her presence at the site had been pretty hard to believe. He'd certainly had the opportunity to kill her. He'd had the facilities to hide her body. He was the last known person to have seen her alive. He'd given an explanation of her disappearance that couldn't be confirmed. He'd given an account of his movements that couldn't be checked. He'd had a motive, now fully revealed, of startling strength. And, last but not least, he'd been virtually accused of murder by an anonymous eye-witness . . .

Even to a cautious man, it was quite a list. Any points in Hunt's favour—and Nield realised there were some—seemed quite overshadowed by the circumstantial case against him. The question now was whether the fen would yield up the proof that was needed.

Chapter Six

Dyson had been waiting there for some time when Nield arrived. He had parked his car beside two large coaches with cards in the windows saying "Field Study Group"; changed into gumboots, and was now sitting on a grassy bank just inside the main entrance of the reserve, reading a *Guide to the Fen* that he'd bought at the warden's cottage. Nield slipped on his own boots, slung a pair of binoculars over his shoulder, and joined the sergeant on the bank. The last traces of mist had dispersed, a pale sun was shining and the day was warm. They'd timed their expedition well.

There was a rough plan of the fen attached to the guide and Nield familiarised himself with its main features before they left. The reserve consisted, it seemed, not of a single fen but of several, each with its separate name. Part of the area was criss-crossed with unbridged dykes and drains and offered no easy means of access except by boat, but a much larger part had been opened up to visitors by the cutting of droves through the reeds and sedge. There were a dozen or more of them, running in various directions and making up an irregular chequer board pattern. They, too, had names. Round the periphery of the opened section, a footpath was marked. Presently the policemen set off along it, crossing a footbridge, skirting a "No Smoking "sign, and continuing in the general direction of the hides.

There was far more activity in the fen than Nield had seen from the caravan site on either of his visits. Near the entrance, a group of students in gumboots and waders, festooned with cameras and weighed down with haversacks and notebooks, were gathered round an elderly man in a deerstalker hat who appeared to be giving a lecture on the habits of water-beetles. Farther along the path there were more students in groups and pairs and singly, bending over plants, sketching leaves and flowers, collecting mosses, photographing specimens. Some of them, Nield noticed, had left the path and penetrated deep into the wet fen, their heads only just visible through the feathery plumes of the reeds that waved in the faint breeze. Two of them were standing in a frozen attitude, watching some bird or animal through field glasses.

Nield began to look worried. He'd expected their task to be difficult—but this place was even more of a wilderness than he'd supposed. It might be a naturalists' paradise, as the guide book said, but it was going to be hell for detectives in search of a body. On both sides of the path there were pools, surrounded by bulrushes, covered with water-lily leaves, difficult of access, and deep. Old peat diggings, the book said—and each a splendid hiding place. The reeds and sedge that stretched away behind them were interlaced with muddy tracks that might or might not have significance. Farther along, there were patches of almost impenetrable scrub, much of it buckthorn, where the sedge fen had been invaded by bushes. The droves themselves proved to be open and grassy, but they too were flanked by acres of reeds, all with their tracks where the researchers had gone in. Nield recalled with dismay the words of the anonymous letter—"I saw a man and a girl walking along one of the droves in the moonlight. I watched them disappear round a bend. ...." But which drove? And which bend? At some point they all had bends. So where to look? The whole county police force could comb this place for weeks, and still find nothing. ...

Dyson was evidently thinking the same thing. "I'd call it a murderer's paradise," he said.

Nield nodded gloomily.

They walked on, gradually leaving the students behind. Presently they came to a sheet of water, an extensive mere with reed beds at its margins, open to the south, tree-lined on the slightly higher ground to the north. They were approaching the hides now. The first tower looked brand new. It was beautifully built, of reed thatch and timber, and sited among the tree trunks and boughs in such a way that from the mere it must have been almost invisible. The door had a padlock on it, and so had a gate in the fence that surrounded it. The older hide, fifty yards on, looked pretty dilapidated. Much of the thatch had fallen away and there was neither fence nor door. Dyson peered inside. The light was poor, but he could see a wooden ladder. He went in, followed cautiously by Nield, and tested the ladder for strength. "Seems all right," he said.

They climbed twenty feet and emerged on to a roofed-in wooden platform. The light was better up above. All round the tower there was a broad, unglazed gap at eye level, interrupted only by the wooden supports that held the roof. The ancient floor groaned and creaked under their tread. It was littered with old thatch and dead leaves, sweet papers and picnic debris.

Dyson looked about him with distaste. "Not my idea of a love nest," he said.

Nield grunted. "At least it's dry. . . ."

They walked slowly round the tower, gazing out through the gap. To the south, there was a fine view over the mere, where birds in great variety were feeding and flying. Just below them, a heron stood motionless. Gulls wheeled and squawked, curlew called plaintively, mallard and teal wove in and out of the reeds. . . . At any other time, Dyson would have asked to borrow Nield's glasses—but not now. . . . They continued their circuit. To the east and the west, the view was largely obscured by the trees. To the north, a wide segment of fen was visible. The path they had just traversed, the reeds and the scrub, the pools. . . .

It was Dyson who pointed in sudden excitement. "Look at that. . . . !"

Nield followed the direction of his pointing finger. Through a tracery of tree branches, a pale green swathe was viable. Part of a drove. . . . And the only bit of drove in sight. . . . All the others, by the accident of angles, were hidden by the reeds. What was more, the drove had a bend in it, which was why only part of it could be seen. And beyond the visible section, in an almost dead straight line, the white of a caravan gleamed.

"Yes . . ." Nield said. It certainly filled the bill—and no other place did. . . . But he was wondering about the distance. It was quite a long way to the bend. Could anyone in the tower really have heard a cry from down there?

"Let's try it out," he said. "You go on ahead, Sergeant. . . . When you get to the bend, give a yell. . . ."

"All right, sir."

"Not *too* loud. . . . I'll join you down there."

Dyson departed. Nield watched him disappear among the trees. For a time he was out of sight. Then, through the glasses, Nield was just able to make out a moving head above the reeds. That would be the part of the drove that was obscured. He turned away, still standing close to the gap but making no special effort to listen. Several minutes passed. He was just beginning to think that Dyson must be out of earshot, that the experiment had failed, when he heard a peculiar but clearly audible cry. . . . Full marks to the letter writer. . . .

He descended the ladder, made his way through the trees to the path, and quickly found the entrance to the drove. There was a name plate at the edge of the reeds—"Stoker's Drove." Running alongside the drove on the left was a twenty-foot-wide dyke of peat-brown water—"Stoker's Dyke". . . .

Dyson was waiting for him, eager and expectant, a little way beyond the bend. "Did you hear me?" he asked.

"Yes, quite clearly. . . ." Nield gazed around in a business-like way. "Right—let's see if we can reconstruct. . . . Hunt would have been walking with the girl from the direction of the caravan site. . . . That would have been along the straight stretch we saw from the hide—so they *would* have been visible in the moonlight. . . . All right so far. . . . Then they rounded this bend—and the reeds cut off the view. . . ." Nield took the letter card from his pocket and consulted it. "'Then I heard the girl give a sort of squeal. . . .'"

"Presumably the moment of murder," Dyson said. "It sounds as though it happened right away."

"Yes. . . . So now he had a body on his hands. . . ." Nield continued to read. "'Later on I saw a torch flashing . . .'—this is where the timing gets vague—'and presently the man went back along the drove by himself'."

"If the time gap was long enough," Dyson said, "he could have been disposing of the body. Burying it. . . . That would account for the torch flashing. . . . Except that he wouldn't have had any tools with him."

"He could have dumped the body and come back later with tools."

"Not those we saw at the site," Dyson said. "They hadn't been used."

"No—but there might have been others hidden away somewhere. . . . Let's see if there's any sign of the reeds having been entered."

They walked slowly along the drove. Dyson's eyes were on the dyke, and the reeds on the other side of it. The man had arrived on foot with the girl—but he could have left a dinghy here earlier and ferried the body across. This dyke obviously joined up with the lode. . . . Nield was studying the ground to the right—"Stoker's Fen," a nameplate said. First, there was a ditch, with very tall reeds growing in it. Beyond was an area of waterlogged peat, with ridges and furrows formed by earlier peat cuttings. Sedge covered the ridges, and reeds flourished in the hollows. Through occasional gaps in the vegetation, Nield caught the glint of water where deep pits had filled.

Suddenly, Dyson called out. "Look here, sir . . . !" He was gazing down into the dyke. Nield joined him. Tied up to an iron mooring spike in the bank there was a punt—a large, flat-bottomed working punt, with long oars and an outboard engine, protected by a piece of oilcloth. On the floor there was a tarpaulin, covering something. Dyson whipped it off. Underneath were two spades and a shovel. One of the spades was dry. The other one, and the shovel, showed traces of wet, black earth on their blades.

"Well, that could be the answer to the tool problem," Dyson said. "Hunt could have known they were here."

Nield nodded. "It begins to add up. . . . So he buried her somewhere. But where?"

"It must be somewhere close," Dyson said. "He'd have wanted to be quick—and he couldn't have asked for a better place."

"All right—let's go over the ground again."

They retraced their steps. Because of the punt, Dyson was now even more interested in the ground across the dyke—but the line of reeds there was continuous and undisturbed. Nield again concentrated on the broken ground to the right, scrutinising every inch for signs of entry, continually parting the upstanding fringe of reeds so that he could peer through. . . . Then, when they were almost back to the bend, he found what he was looking for. Through a gap in the reeds, a footmark. . . . And another . . . Footmarks leading away into the fen. . . .

Nield stepped carefully across the ditch and examined the nearest of the marks. In the squelchy ground it was no more than a deep and shapeless hole—obviously a footprint, but with collapsed sides. It could have been made by anyone's feet. And the marks beyond it were the same.

"Come on in," Nield said. "We can't do any damage."

He set off through the reeds, with Dyson following close behind. Almost at once, he stopped. To the left, there was a flattened patch of vegetation. "Looks as though something might have been put down there," he said.

Dyson nodded. "That makes sense, too. . . . Hunt would have needed overalls and gumboots—and he couldn't have had them with him. . . . He could have put the body here temporarily, while he fetched them. This would have been where the torch flashes were seen. . . . By the time he got back, the fellow in the hide would have gone."

"Yes—that fits. . . ."

Nield moved on. The track ahead was unmistakable—a line of deep holes where feet had sunk, a parting of the reeds and sedge, a trail of broken leaves and stalks. . . . Twenty yards on, the track abruptly ended. Looking over the top of the reeds, Nield saw in front of him a piece of open water—a small pond. A pair of mallard duck rose squawking at the sight of him and flapped away. . . . At his feet, there was a small clearing—an oval of almost bare black mud with a film of water over it. The oval was about six feet long by three feet wide.

Dyson stared grimly down at it. "Looks like the end of the road, sir."

"Yes," Nield said.

The sergeant turned away. "I'll get the tools."

"We'd better make do with the dry spade," Nield called after him. "There may be prints on the others."

"Right . . ."

Dyson was back in a few moments. Neither man said anything more. It was a ghastly job that had to be done—and the sooner it was over the better. Dyson gave his jacket to Nield, and rolled up his sleeves. Then he thrust the spade into the soil at about the centre of the oval. The ground had been so trodden down and impacted that it was almost as resistant as unturned earth. Bruised leaves and roots impeded the blade. Black water seeped into the hole left by the digging, obstructing the view. Mud shot up in fountains.

For several minutes, Dyson worked in silence, clearing the top spit. Then, as he thrust deeper, the spade struck something more solid than roots. He bent and put his hand into the hole, feeling around. There was something smooth and narrow—like a bare arm—a wrist. . . .

Sweat broke out on his forehead. Under the mud splashes, his face paled. He had known plenty of horrors in his police work—but nothing quite as upsetting as this. He had too much imagination. That beautiful hair, that lovely face—and in this filth. . . . He braced himself. No point in thinking about it. Better get it over. He cleared more earth away, and plunged his hand into the hole again, and pulled gently on the thing he'd touched. The black mud heaved—and suddenly the object shot out with a sucking noise. A piece of smooth dark wood. . . .

"Bog oak," Dyson said, wiping the sweat from his face with the back of a muddy hand.

He continued to dig. Soon he had uncovered all the centre part of the oval to a depth of eighteen inches or more. At that depth he met resistance again. Once more he thrust his arm down, following the contours of the object, scraping the mud away from it with his fingers. Slowly, the expression on his face changed from revulsion to astonishment.

"It's more bog oak," he said. "A great solid lump of it. . . . And it goes right across. . . . No one's dug below that." He straightened up. "We were wrong, sir. . . . There's nothing here."

Nield passed Dyson his jacket. Dyson struggled into it. Both men stared down at the hole in perplexity.

"I don't get it," Dyson said "The body *ought* to be here. This is the place—everything points to it. . . . The *only* place that fits the letter. . . . I'll swear no one's entered the fen at any other point round here. We combed every inch."

Nield grunted.

Suddenly Dyson said, "Maybe he buried it here first—and then moved it to an entirely different spot . . . He could have got the wind up after we showed him the letter. He'd have guessed we'd be down here searching. I'll bet that's what happened."

"When do you suggest he moved it?"

"Well—last night. He couldn't have done it any other time."

Nield shook his head. "There was a thick mist last night. He wouldn't have been able to see a thing."

"If he was desperate enough, he'd have managed somehow."

"No, Sergeant—I don't believe it. Visibility was only a yard or two. Even if he'd been able to find the place again, which I doubt, he'd have blundered about in the reeds, made new tracks, left traces everywhere. . . . Especially carrying a body. . . . I'm certain he didn't come back last night."

"Then I don't understand it," Dyson said. "If Hunt didn't dig a grave here, how do you account for all the mess—the bare patch. . . . Someone's spent a lot of time here."

"It could have been one of those naturalists—like the two we saw standing out in the fen this afternoon. He could have been watching the birds on the pond through there—using the spot as a sort of hide. The place probably would have looked like a trampled grave by the time he'd finished. . . . Could you swear the ground had ever been dug up?"

"No—not for sure."

"Well, there you are. . . . I'm afraid we've been led astray."

"By the letter."

"Yes. . . . Maybe Hunt was right after all. . . . Maybe all the fellow saw from the hide was an ordinary couple—strolling, sky-larking, then separating. . . ."

"And there just happened to be a track here?"

"Why not? We know they're all over the fen."

"That's true. . . ." Wearily, Dyson picked up his spade, "So what's the next move, sir?"

"For you," Nield said, "a hot bath. . . . You should see yourself!"

Chapter Seven

At approximately the time that Nield and Dyson were trudging back to their cars through the fen, Alan Hunt was telephoning his fiancée at the Crown Hotel.

Susan Ainger had returned the previous evening from her expedition to London. Hunt had already talked to her once on the phone, asking about the shopping she'd done, the people she'd visited, the comfort of the hotel she'd stayed at, and in general showing himself an affectionate and interested husband-to-be. He had also arranged with her that he should dine at the Aingers' on the following day—which, in part, was why he was now calling her.

"Darling," he said, "I'm afraid I won't be able to have dinner with you this evening after all. Something's come up. . . ."

"Oh, Alan, what a bore!"

"Isn't it. . . .? I very much want to see you, though. Could we meet for an hour on your way home?"

"I expect so," Susan said. "Usual time and place?"

"Yes—Hayes Corner at a quarter past six."

"What's happened—work?"

"No, it's something else. . . . I'll tell you when we meet."

"All right, darling," Susan said. "I won't be late."

She was already at the wood when Hunt arrived. He parked his car under the trees and joined her in the Austin Healey. His brow was furrowed, his manner unaccustomedly diffident. "Hallo, sweetie," he said. He kissed her with much less than his usual ardour—then held her away from him, looking into her eyes. "Susan, I must tell you what's happened."

"If that's the best you can do after three days away from me," she said, "you certainly must!"

"It's no joking matter," he told her. "I'm actually in a bit of a spot."

Her teasing smile faded. "Oh, Alan, I'm sorry. . . . What's happened?"

"It's quite a saga," he said. "It started on Saturday, just after you'd gone away. . . ."

He plunged into his story. Substantially, it was the one he'd told Nield on the Monday morning—but now his manner was less light-hearted, less detached. Susan listened with fascinated interest to his tale of the unexpected visit of a girl he'd met on holiday; of the mix-up in identity that had brought it about; of how the girl was going to have someone's baby; and of her state of mind when she'd found out how she'd been deceived. Hunt described his efforts to persuade her to go home, and how he'd finally succeeded, and how he'd hardly known the girl and had simply been doing her a good turn because she was in trouble. He spoke in a slightly rueful way, keeping the story brief and matter-of-fact, watching Susan all the time to see how she was taking it.

She took the facts unquestioningly, with naïve faith. "Poor girl," she said. "And what an awful bind for you. . . . But I must say you seem to have done jolly well. Why do you say you're in a spot?"

"Well, darling, it seems the girl didn't actually *get* home . . ." Hunt explained how he'd set her down a little way short of her house, and why. "She must have changed her mind again at the last minute and gone off. . . . And yesterday morning the police came to see me."

"The police! About her. . . .?"

"Yes. . . . They wanted to know what I'd done with her. . . . ! It's so fantastic, Susan, I can hardly believe it. . . . From what they said, they seemed to think it was *I* who'd got the girl pregnant—and that I hadn't taken her to Peterborough at all. They behaved just as though they suspected me of having bumped her off."

Susan stared at him. "They must be out of their minds."

"That's what I said. . . . Of course, in a way I can understand their point of view. The girl had disappeared, and I can't *prove* I took her to Peterborough. I can't prove anything, really. . . . And there's another stupid thing that cropped up, too—it couldn't have come at a worse moment. . . ."

"What's that?"

"Well, apparently some busybody was in Ocken Fen on Saturday night and he saw a man and a girl together and heard the girl cry out and he sent the police a note about it. Anonymously—he hadn't even the guts to sign his name. It was probably just a couple fooling about, but he made it sound terribly sinister—said the man went off on his own after flashing a torch around. . . . The trouble is, he said he thought the man looked a bit like me. Just *thought*, mind you—but it didn't stop him throwing accusations about . . . So now you can see why I'm in a jam."

"I've never heard anything so ridiculous," Susan said. For the first time ever, Hunt saw her looking angry.

"I know. . . . It just shows how a completely innocent person *can* get caught up in these things—and how difficult it is to clear yourself. . . . I've told the police exactly what happened—but the trouble is they don't *know* me. So they don't know whether to believe me or not. To them, I'm just a man who came up with a rather extraordinary story he can't substantiate. A man with a motive, too—they seem to think I might have got rid of the girl because she could have got in the way of my marrying you. . . . I suppose it's their duty to be suspicious and think up every nasty angle they can—bat it's damned unpleasant for me."

"Darling, it's *horrible* for you—it's a perfectly awful thing to have happened. I'm livid about it. . . ." She sat silent for a moment, considering the situation. "Still," she said, "once the girl turns up, that'll be the end of it, won't it?"

"Oh, yes—as long as she does turn up. If she doesn't, things might get a bit rugged—and she *did* talk of losing herself. . . . But I'm not worried about the long term—the police are pretty certain to dig up some bit of evidence that proves my story. . . . What worries me is what's going to happen in the next few days."

"What do you mean?"

"Well, there'll obviously be a search for the girl, and that means the newspapers will have to be told all about the case. . . . When the story comes out, it's going to look pretty bad for me. I'm afraid a lot of people are going to suspect me. In fact, my name's going to be mud around here for a bit."

A little of the colour went out of Susan's cheeks. "Well, I call that most unfair," she said indignantly; "It's not *your* fault that the girl came to see you—and all you did was try to help her."

"*I* know that," Hunt said, "and you know it—but is the world going to believe it? I'm afraid I'm in for a rather sticky time. . . ." He reached for Susan's hand. "I'm so sorry it's happened, sweetie. . . . It's going to be beastly for you, too."

"You don't have to worry about me," Susan said.

"But I do, Susan—terribly. I love you so much—I wouldn't have involved you in a sordid thing like this for anything in the world. . . . Now that I have, I wouldn't blame you if you felt you couldn't go through with our marriage. Or at least if you wanted to postpone it. . . ."

"Alan. . . . ! You're not serious?"

"I am serious. . . . It would just about break my heart if you called it off, but I certainly don't feel I've any right to hold you to a promise you made when things were so different. . . . The least I can do is offer you your freedom."

"Heavens, you do sound old-fashioned. . . . ! I don't want my freedom—I only wish we could get married to-morrow. . . . In any case, I wouldn't call it off now—what sort of a person do you take me for? You don't really suppose I'd leave you in the lurch just when you need me most?"

"That's not how I'd think of it, Susan. I'd think you were being sensible. . . . I'm not sure you realise, yet, just how unpleasant it's going to be."

"I don't care *what* it's like," Susan said. "If you're in a jam, I'd much sooner be in it with you. . . . Now will you please stop talking nonsense."

Hunt sighed. "You're so loyal, darling. . . . I only hope you won't regret it."

91

"Of course I won't."

He bent and kissed her. "I love you very much, Susan—and I don't want you to be hurt. If you should change your mind later on. . . ."

"*Please*, Alan!"

"Very well—I won't say anything more. . . . We'll just have to hope they find the girl quickly."

Susan nodded. "Hadn't we better tell Daddy about all this?"

"We must, of course. . . . I'll tell him myself, it's my job. . . . But I think I'll wait a day or two—there's no point in upsetting him and your mother before it's necessary—and if the girl's found soon, it won't be. Don't you agree?"

"Yes, all right. . . . When am I going to see you again?"

"Well, it may not be too easy for the next couple of days—I'm supposed to be holding myself available at the site for questioning. I shouldn't really have slipped away this evening. . . . But I'll ring you each day, and tell you the news."

"Twice a day, please. . . ."

Hunt smiled. "Okay—twice a day. . . . Darling, I can't tell you how much better you've made me feel. I'm sure this trouble will soon pass—and we'll get married and live happily ever after. . . . Right?"

Susan nodded. "I love you so much, Alan. . . ." She smiled a little, too. "I even love you for wanting to 'give me my freedom'. . . . !"

Chapter Eight

Nield spent the evening in a major reappraisal of the case.

For a short time in the fen, he'd felt grimly sure that Hunt was in fact Gwenda Nicholls's murderer. The proof had seemed almost within his grasp. ... Now he was far from sure. The suggestion behind the anonymous letter—the strongest evidence for murder and the strongest evidence against Hunt—had proved baseless. There had been no foul play at that spot. The writer *had* been mistaken. The letter had therefore lost all its relevance—and the case was transformed. If a body had not been buried at the place the letter indicated, there was really no reason to suppose that a body had been buried anywhere—or, indeed, that there *was* a body. ... Certainly there was no firm evidence. ... So now the other possibility had to be considered.

Nield's thoughts switched back to Gwenda Nicholls. Who could tell what might have passed through her mind on that journey to Peterborough?—assuming the journey had been made. So much turned on what she was really like. Hunt's picture had been of an emotional, unstable, desperate girl. The parents hadn't recognised the picture. Which of them had been right? Parents, particularly the strait and narrow ones, were sometimes the last to know their children. If Gwenda had been unstable, she *might* have changed her mind again. At the last moment, she might have found the ordeal of confession more than she could face. Her parents had seemed kind enough at heart—but there would certainly have been a terrible scene. Anger and tears, bitter denunciations, endless questioning—and afterwards, perhaps, a constant reverting, an intolerable nagging. ... It was all very well for the parents to say they would have helped—but on what terms? Generous, ungrudging, genuinely forgiving—or humiliating. ...? Perhaps Gwenda had known them better than they knew themselves. ... She might have preferred at least to postpone the ordeal. She might have gone off temporarily, to think over what she would say, to explore some alternative. If she had decided to do that, she would understandably not have told Hunt in the car, for fear he would try to dissuade her again. And it would explain why she hadn't wanted him to drive her up to the house. ... It was possible. ...

Then there was Hunt himself. ... Assuming murder had been done, there was still a circumstantial case against him—even disregarding the letter. There was the motive and the opportunity and the disappearance. ... But now Nield wondered if he'd paid enough attention to the points in Hunt's favour. Some were minor, some were negative—but together they made up quite a defence. Nield mentally listed them—as earlier he'd listed the points for the prosecution. ...

Nothing in Hunt's remarkable story had been disproved. He hadn't been caught out in any lies. There wasn't the slightest evidence that he'd seduced Gwenda. On the contrary, her parents had been sure that he'd had almost no contact with her. The fact that she hadn't seen him off when he'd left the hotel seemed to bear that out. A girl who'd had an intimate holiday affair would surely have been present on the quay, however discreetly. ... And it certainly wasn't beyond the bounds of possibility that the real seducer had given Hunt's address to the girl. There were types who'd have thought that amusing. ...

As for the trip to Peterborough, it *could* have happened. Indeed, Nield reflected, there was a kind of evidence that it had. The girl's telephone call to the Bakers' had to be taken into account here. After all, she'd made it herself, and presumably of her own free will. If she'd decided to let Hunt take her home, it was fully explained. But otherwise, why would she have made it . . .? A tricky point—but surely in Hunt's favour. . . .?

Then there was Hunt's general manner. He'd shown not a trace of guilt at any time. In fact, in the early stages he'd appeared quite carefree. Nield found it hard to believe that he'd have been quite so nonchalant at that first interview if he'd murdered a girl over the week-end. Fear, if not conscience, would have led to over-acting—and Hunt's manner had been exactly right. The arrival of the police car certainly hadn't bothered him at all. Later on, he'd become worried and angry—but that was natural, considering what he stood to lose from wrongful suspicion. Looking back, Nield could find no fault with his demeanour at any point. He'd been completely frank—to the point of lunacy, if he'd been guilty. He hadn't *had* to say that Gwenda was pregnant—he could easily have thought of some other explanation for her call. . . .He hadn't *had* to stress his eagerness to marry Susan Ainger—to volunteer the information that he'd worked in Norwich and changed his job to be near her. . . . Again, he'd missed opportunities that a guilty man would surely have taken. That question he'd been asked about Gwenda's state of mind in the car, for instance. He could, easily have attributed a few words to her which would have supported the idea that she might have been backsliding. Instead, he'd merely said she was gloomy. . . .

Finally, there was the total lack of material evidence. No trace of blood on any clothing, no signs of violence anywhere. . . . Of course, you could have murder without blood. If Hunt had strangled the girl—and with a powerful man and a slightly-built woman it was the obvious method—there'd have been no blood. But in that case Nield would have expected to find scratches on him. A choking girl would claw wildly. . . . And there'd been no scratches. Gloves could have taken care of the hands—though not those heavy gloves in the caravan, they'd have been too clumsy. . . . Other gloves, perhaps. . . . But there was still the unmarked face. . . .

Uneasily, Nield looked back on his handling of the case. Perhaps he'd been concentrating too much on trying to disprove Hunt's story—because of the letter—and not enough on trying to confirm it. Gwenda Nicholls *could* have disappeared voluntarily. Hunt could have been telling the truth. The time had come to seek positive evidence on both points. . . .

First, the disappearance. . . . Nield was at his office at an early hour next morning, organising a "missing person" drive on a basis of urgency. Much of the work was routine . . . Reproduction of Gwenda's picture in large numbers. . . . Description and photograph to all police stations by the usual channels. . . . Ditto to all national newspapers, and those local ones serving the East Anglian area—with all available information about the girl's last known movements. . . . Ditto to the B.B.C. and the other TV networks. . . . Special inquiries to be instituted in Peterborough itself . . .

Next, Hunt's story—and in the first place, the movements of his car. . . . Had anyone seen it parked near the corner of Everton Road soon after eight-thirty on the Saturday evening. A smart, cream MG sports in a quiet suburban road shouldn't have been entirely inconspicuous, and an appeal to the public might bring results . . . More requests to radio and TV, and to the local papers . . . It might be worth asking, too, if any of the villagers at Ocken had seen or heard the car leave or return to the caravan site that Saturday evening. P.C. Blake could look into that. . . .

What else in Hunt's story was subject to checking? The Norway end—there might be something there. Some line on the possible identity of the real seducer, if Hunt wasn't the man. . . .? A long shot, but worth trying. The Norwegian police could be asked to get a list from the hotel of all British male guests whose stay there had overlapped with the Nichollses'. Then the names and addresses could be followed up at home. . . . Not that any man would readily admit to the police that he'd seduced a girl and given someone else's address—especially a girl whose disappearance would soon be widely publicised, who might even have killed herself. But some view might be formed after questioning. . . . Better to have the list, anyway. Nield drafted a message and dispatched it to Oslo.

Now for the local check-up. . . .

"I think, Sergeant," Nield said, "it would be as well if you made the initial Peterborough inquiries yourself—you know the set-up, and it'll save time. . . . Will you get over there right away?"

Dyson nodded.

"Drop in on the parents first and let them know what we're up to—they'll get a shock, otherwise, if they see the girl's face on the telly. . . . Then inquire at all the exit points—and make as much stir as you can. Take plenty of photographs with you—and don't forget about the suitcase she was carrying, and the way she was dressed. With her looks and appearance she must have been pretty striking. . . . Okay?"

"All right," Dyson said. "I'll keep in touch."

A bit of a rift had opened between the two policemen since their abortive expedition to the fen—marked on Nield's part by a slight irritation and a tendency to underline the obvious and on Dyson's by a slight sullenness.

Nield had fully explained to Dyson the grounds for his reappraisal. Dyson had argued about some of them. The picture of Gwenda's supposed mental attitude to her parents, of her renewed agitation at the last moment, had failed to convince him. The fact that Hunt had told of Gwenda's pregnancy could surely be explained by his need to supply a satisfying reason for her voluntary disappearance. The fact that he'd stressed his eagerness to marry Susan Ainger amounted to little—since the purpose of his move from Norwich would have emerged sooner or later in any case. . . . But, in general, Dyson had been obliged to concede much substance in Nield's points. . . .

All the same, he had no enthusiasm for the new direction the inquiry had taken. Maybe he *was* prejudiced against Hunt, as Nield had charged. Dyson preferred to call it a hunch. It wasn't true that he'd completely made up his mind about the man at that moment of reckless driving in Ocken village—but he'd seen him then as a taker of risks and a man of swift reactions—two qualities of any successful plotter and murderer. From that moment he'd disliked and distrusted him—and everything that had happened since had strengthened his feelings.

He couldn't accept, as Nield did, that the anonymous letter was no longer relevant. He wasn't persuaded, as Nield was, that Hunt couldn't have moved the body from its shallow grave on a misty night without leaving signs. In Hunt's place, with a life sentence hanging over him and twelve hours of darkness in which to operate, he felt he would have managed it somehow.

In short, he didn't believe that Gwenda Nicholls was still alive—much as he'd have liked to. He didn't believe that she'd ever been back to Peterborough, and he expected nothing from the national hue and cry that had now been started. . . . Nevertheless, being a policeman still, and a sergeant under orders from a chief inspector, he would do his duty. He would conduct his own inquiries with as much zeal and efficiency as though he'd been hopeful of success.

He went first, as instructed, to Everton Road. Mr. Nicholls was back at work, but Mrs. Nicholls was in. Dyson told her of the nation-wide search for her daughter that had now begun, carefully avoiding any nuance of word or expression that would diminish her hopes. He left as soon as he could.

From Everton Road, he drove to the railway station. None of the staff he talked to there remembered the girl. Saturday night was always a busy one, he was told—she might have passed through or she might not. Before leaving, he noted the routes and stops and destinations of all the trains that had left Peterborough after 8.30 p.m. that night. Special inquiries could be made later along the lines.

From the station, he went to the bus terminal. The problem there was even more difficult. On Saturday night, most of the city's buses would have been crowded—and the girl could have boarded one at any point and been lost in the throng. Dyson talked to conductors, pinned up a photograph and description of Gwenda in the canteen where the busmen rested, and enlisted the help of a couple of inspectors to pursue the matter throughout the day.

From there he moved on to the taxi ranks, the hotels, the coffee bars, the pubs and restaurants, scattering his photographs. Slowly, a deep depression descended on him. Not because of the negative answers, which he'd expected—but because of the picture. The girl's face, with its charming smile and its freshness, enormously appealed to him. Every time he showed it to someone else, he

found himself studying it again—and hating Hunt more than ever.
. . .

By nightfall he was exhausted. But he'd left his mark on Peterborough—and the questions he'd asked wouldn't end with the people he'd met. The search, pointless or not, was on. . . .

Chapter Nine

National interest in the case began to build up from the moment Gwenda Nicholls's picture was flashed on television screens that evening. Within minutes, Nield and Dyson and the special staff they'd organised were taking telephone calls from people who believed they'd seen the girl. This was the usual result of a "missing person" appeal, and it raised no hopes. Many of the reports were too vague to be helpful; some were from obvious crackpots; a few seemed worth following up. As Nield had expected, the supposed sightings were taking place in widely scattered parts of the country, and nearly all the field work had to be passed to the various local forces.

The first public references to Hunt came with the morning newspapers. The quality papers had contented themselves with printing Gwenda's photograph and description, but several of the popular papers mentioned her visit to Ocken. The *Record's* report was the starkest. Miss Nicholls, it said, had spent the Saturday afternoon and evening with Mr. Alan Hunt, sales manager at the Cosy Caravan site, Ocken, and had subsequently been driven by him to Peterborough, where she lived. Nothing further had been heard of her.

During the morning, a dozen newspapers rang up Nield or sent reporters. He told them that no hard news of the girl had yet come in; declined to enlarge on the previous day's official hand-out; sidestepped questions about the possibility of "foul play", which was naturally in their minds in view of all the fuss; and referred them to Hunt for further information about Saturday's events. He said nothing about the anonymous letter.

It was in the evening papers that the story of the "Missing Redhead" hit the headlines in a big way. By now there had been time for interviews—with the Nichollses, with the Bakers, with Hunt himself—and the drawing of conclusions from the mounting facts. Gwenda's parents had talked very little, confining themselves to saying what a good daughter Gwenda had been and how anxious they were that she should return home. Hunt, on the other hand, had talked a great deal. His account of what had happened differed in language from what he'd told the inspector, but in substance it was the same—and what with the seduction, the pregnancy, and the mysterious disappearance, it made splendid copy. He'd evidently had to answer a lot of questions, and some of them had been probing—but his honest perplexity came out in the printed word as it had in conversation. . . . All the same, his photograph in one of the papers was captioned "The Man Who Saw Her Last," while another one had a significantly detailed paragraph about Susan Ainger, "Mr. Hunt's Fiancée," with a picture of Copper Beeches and a gossipy item about Henry Ainger and his thriving property companies. A local paper had revived the "Newmarket Heiress" story and caption. The Press, like the police, had obviously found Hunt's story remarkable. None of the papers mentioned the anonymous letter. Hunt, too, had kept quiet about that.

Telephone calls continued to pour into Nield's headquarters all through the afternoon and evening. One was from Hunt, sounding more perturbed than ever and asking anxiously if there was any news of Gwenda. Another was from Mr. Nicholls, who'd just read about Hunt's fiancée in the papers and noted the snide captions and was in a state of great distress. Nield soothed him as best he could. In the early evening a report came through that seemed to offer a ray of hope—a ticket collector at Stamford thought he remembered a girl getting off a Peterborough train who had answered to the description circulated. But a subsequent check established that it had been someone else. Nothing came in from Peterborough itself. No one reported having seen a cream MG sports car standing in Everton Road. From P.C. Blake came a message that he'd been unable to find anyone in Ocken who'd seen or heard the cream car on the move on the Saturday evening. Though, as Nield said, a negative report like that had little value. . . .

Around seven o'clock, a telegram arrived from the Norwegian police. The Vistasund Hotel, it said, was now closed for the winter. The proprietor had gone to America, and the staff was dispersed. An answer to Nield's inquiry would be sent as soon as possible, but getting the information would take time.

"Blanks all round," Nield said gloomily. With only short breaks, he and Dyson had been working continuously for thirty-six hours, and both of them were feeling pretty tired. Dyson hadn't even had Nield's hope to buoy him up, and looked as though he might hand in his resignation at any moment.

"You'd better get some food, Sergeant," Nield said.

At that moment there was a disturbance in the outer lobby—the sound of a raised voice, and fierce argument. A young constable looked in. "Are you free, sir?" he asked Nield. "There's a man who . . ."

Before he could make an announcement, someone brushed past him. A short, stocky man, with a sheaf of papers under his arm, and a blazing face. He stormed up to Nield. "Are you the inspector in charge of the Gwenda Nicholls case?"

"I am," Nield said.

"Then I'd like a word with you in private. . . . My name's Henry Ainger."

Chapter Ten

Nield studied him for a moment. "I see, sir . . . Well, you'd better come into my office." He led the way into an inner room and drew out a chair for his visitor.

Ainger ignored it. "What the hell do you think you're up to, Inspector?"

"I'm looking for a missing girl," Nield said quietly.

"That's not all you're doing. . . ." Ainger slapped his newspapers down on the desk. "Look at this—and this . . . ! 'The last man to see her . . .' 'Helping the police with their inquiries . . .' You know what that phrase is intended to mean—and so do I. They're accusing Alan Hunt of murder."

"I think that's a slight exaggeration," Nield said. "In any case, I'm not responsible for what the newspapers say."

"You gave them the information that set them off."

"A girl is missing," Nield repeated. "What would you expect me to do—keep quiet about it . . .? Of course I gave them the information."

"You didn't have to bring Hunt into it."

"I didn't bring him into it more than I could help," Nield said. "I was careful not to. But when you start a search you have to mention the missing person's last known movements. I gave the Press the necessary facts—no more, no less. . . . Most of this stuff in the papers comes from Hunt himself. It was up to him whether he talked or not."

"He didn't have much choice, once you'd set the pack on him . . . It's character-assassination. It's a bloody outrage . . ."

Nield's mouth tightened. "Now look, Mr. Ainger, this attitude isn't going to get you anywhere. I understand how you feel, and I sympathise. You're deeply concerned in this and I'm quite ready to discuss the situation with you . . ."

"I should damned well think so."

". . . in a reasonable way," Nield said. "But if you're going to be abusive, I shall have you shown out. Is that clear . . .? Now I suggest you sit down."

Fuming, Ainger dropped into the chair. The inspector took his accustomed seat behind the desk.

"I assume," Nield said, "that by now you've had a full account of everything from Hunt."

"I have—I've just spent two hours with him—and with my daughter. . . . The most fantastic two hours I ever spent in my life. . . . He told me you suspected him of seducing Gwenda Nicholls on holiday, killing her because she was pregnant, and inventing a phoney story to cover it all up."

"I wouldn't put it as strongly as that," Nield said. "I've been going into the possibility. . . ."

"Put it how you like—the result's just as unpleasant for him . . . Now where's the evidence? He mentioned some anonymous letter. I'd like to see it."

Nield took a photostat of the letter from a drawer and passed it across the table.

Ainger read it through, scowling. "You regard this as evidence?"

"I think it had to be looked into."

"Did you look into it? Did you try to check on what it says?"

Nield nodded. "By good luck, we were able to identify the place mentioned in the letter. We searched for a body. There was nothing."

"So the writer was wrong?"

"Apparently."

"That takes care of the letter, then . . ." Ainger flung it down contemptuously. "So now what makes you think the girl is dead?"

"I don't know whether she's dead or not," Nield said. "All I know is that she's been missing for five days."

"How long have you been actively searching for her?"

"Only for about thirty-six hours—but she has a striking

appearance, and with the whole country alerted I'd have hoped for some line on her by now. Unless she's deliberately hiding away. . . ."

"Wasn't that precisely her idea. . . .? If she's changed her name, her clothes, her hair style, would you still expect to find her?"

"It would certainly be much more difficult," Nield said.

"And that could have happened?"

"It could have done."

"Aren't your records full of missing persons who've never been traced? Don't people often disappear voluntarily, for all sorts of reasons?"

"They do. . . . I assure you I haven't ruled out the possibility in Gwenda Nicholls's case."

Ainger snorted. "But meanwhile, Hunt takes the rap. . . . ! Have you any good reason to doubt that he drove the girl to Peterborough as he said?"

"No . . . But I've no proof, either."

"I've no proof that I drove here via Newmarket—but I did . . . What about factual evidence? Have you found anything suspicious at his place? Any clues that point to him as a murderer?"

"No—nothing."

"Have you caught him out in any lies? Has he been obstructive?"

"No—he's been very frank and above-board."

"Then I'm baffled, Inspector. . . . What *have* you got against him?"

Nield stirred uneasily. "It must be obvious to you, sir, why we've made inquiries. . . . The girl is missing, Hunt was the last known person to see her, he told an extraordinary story which can't be confirmed—and he could have had a very strong motive for getting rid of her."

"He wanted to marry my daughter, you mean?"

"Exactly. I gather she's a well-to-do young woman in her own right."

"A man isn't necessarily a criminal," Ainger said "because he wants to marry a woman who happens to have money. . . . I should know—I did it myself, and for the best of reasons—I was fond of the girl . . . Naturally, when Hunt first appeared on the scene it did occur to me that he might be a grabber—so I studied him carefully. I decided he wasn't—and I was right. The other day he turned down an offer I made him of a first-class job, because he preferred to be independent. And when this trouble blew up he thought he ought to end his engagement to my daughter. Would he have done that if he'd been an unscrupulous fortune-hunter?"

Nield looked surprised. "*Has* he ended it?"

"He hasn't, but only because Susan flatly refused to let him. He tried—he tried very hard. . . . So there's your motive blown sky high—like everything else. . . . For God's sake, Inspector, where's your case?"

Nield sighed wearily. "You don't seem to understand, sir. I never said there was a case. I've made no accusations. I'm too aware of the points that can be made in Hunt's favour—and there are far more of them, incidentally, than you've mentioned yourself . . . All I've done is look into things. That's my duty."

"*Duty* . . . ! You've blackened a young man's reputation, you've destroyed a girl's happiness, you've wrecked the peace of a household—and all without a single shred of evidence. What sort of duty is that?"

"Unfortunately," Nield said, "it's often impossible to investigate a case of this kind without some suspicion falling temporarily on innocent people . . . It's hard—but it's unavoidable . . . If Hunt has come under public suspicion, and he's innocent, I'm very sorry about it—sincerely sorry. But for the time being, there's nothing I can do."

"You can tell the Press there's no justification for their treatment of him. You can exonerate him."

Nield shook his head. "I can't exonerate him, any more than I can accuse him. If I could, I'd be only too glad to. At the moments I've no grounds for either course. . . ."

Ainger pushed back his chair. "Well, that may satisfy you, Inspector, but it doesn't satisfy me. It's not justice. I thought a man was supposed to be considered innocent till he was proved guilty. . . . Evidently I was wrong. What you're doing is punishing Hunt, and everyone associated with him, for something he didn't do—and you're not going to get away with it. I shall advise him to sue you, and the newspapers, for defamation—and I'll back him to the hilt."

Nield gave a curt nod. "That's your privilege, Mr. Ainger. You won't, I'm sure, expect me to change my attitude because of threats. . . ." He opened the door. "Good-bye, sir."

Chapter Eleven

Nield slept badly that night.

Normally, he didn't allow his professional problems to keep him awake—he'd realised long ago that lying in bed and worrying about them didn't help. He'd learned to discipline himself—to switch off, and start again fresh next day. It always paid. . . .

This time, though, he couldn't switch off. He was overtired, he decided. Maybe getting a bit old for the job, with its long hours, its tremendous responsibilities, its pressures . . . Or was this just an exceptionally difficult and complex case? He certainly felt very dissatisfied with the way it had gone. There were so few anchor points he could refer to with confidence—so few facts. Apart from Hunt's story, he'd had almost nothing to go on. And the prospects looked no better. The only end he could see to the case was a question mark—unless he could find the girl, dead or alive. . . . Or establish her voluntary disappearance. . . .

The interview with Ainger, too, had upset him. Not because of the threat of a court action—that was just angry talk, which he was used to. The police were constantly being threatened by people who relied on their protection and resented the only methods by which it could be achieved. . . . But Nield was a humane man with a conscience, and he didn't like what had happened in this case any more than Ainger did. The lives of several people *were* being undermined by suspicion and uncertainty—and there *wasn't* any real evidence against Hunt. There was only a doubt. . . .

It was a pity, Nield thought, that Hunt had talked so freely to the Press about Gwenda and the purpose of her visit, about the alleged seducer, about his own marriage plans. If he'd been a little more discreet, there wouldn't have been nearly such a fuss. He'd positively invited public suspicion. But there again—wasn't indiscretion on that scale a sure mark of innocence? What guilty man would so determinedly have marshalled the facts against himself. . . .?

Nield was wrong about the prospects. The morning was to bring a sensational transformation of the case.

He surfaced from the restless dozing of the night with a headache and a muzzy mind. He swallowed the aspirin his wife brought him, bathed and shaved, and went gloomily down to breakfast. He'd barely glanced at the headlines in the *Telegraph* when the phone rang.

"Inspector Nield?" a voice said. "Ah—morning, sir. It's the station sergeant, Peterborough, here. . . ."

Nield felt a surge of hope. "What is it—news of the girl?"

"No, sir. . . . But I've got a couple of people here who say they saw a cream MG sports car parked near Everton Road on Saturday evening."

"Good lord," Nield exclaimed. "All right, Sergeant—keep them there . . . Tell them I'm on my way to see them."

It was ninety minutes later when Nield and Dyson strode into Peterborough police headquarters.

"They're in the waiting room, sir," the station sergeant said. "Getting a bit restive. . . . A Mr. John Porter and his girl friend, Miss Margery Haines. He's a bank clerk, she's a secretary. They both live close by Everton Road. . . . They heard the appeal on the radio."

"Thanks, Sergeant . . ." Nield led the way into the waiting room. A young man in his middle twenties rose as the policemen entered. He looked a solid, respectable type. The girl was younger, well-groomed, easy on the eye. Nield introduced himself, and apologised for keeping them. "If you'll give me your office numbers I'll make it right with your employers," he said. "Now—tell me about this car."

"It was a cream MG sports," Porter said. "It was parked in

Grange Road, just round the corner from Everton Road, by a telephone box."

"What time was this?"

"About twenty to nine on Saturday evening."

"You're sure of that?"

"Yes—my fiancée was telephoning and she was rather a long time—so I looked at my watch."

"Did you see who was in the car?"

"Yes—a man on his own. A hefty chap, fair hair, about thirty."

"You noticed all that in the dark?"

"He was parked under a lamp," Porter said. "And I'd plenty of time to look at him while I was waiting."

"What was he doing?"

"Nothing special. Just sitting and smoking a cigarette."

Nield produced a newspaper photograph of Hunt. "Is that the man?"

Porter gave it one glance. "Yes—that's him."

"You're sure?"

"Absolutely certain."

"What about you, Miss Haines?"

"It looks like him," she said.

"I see. . . . Well, I'd like to have your home addresses, if I may. . . . And thank you both for coming forward—it was very public-spirited of you, and you've done a most useful job . . ."

As they left, Nield looked quizzically at Dyson. "Well, Sergeant—any comment?"

Dyson gave a faint shrug. "It seems he was there . . . I must say I'm very surprised."

"*I'm* extremely thankful," Nield said. His headache was clearing—he was beginning to feel much more human. "It's exactly the confirmation we've been wanting—and if he told the truth about that, we've no reason to doubt the rest of his story. I'd say he's in the clear. He dropped the girl as he told us, she wandered off and went to ground—and that's it . . . No foul play, no suspicion of anyone . . . Case virtually over."

Dyson grunted.

"You doubt it, Sergeant?"

"I'm not too sure about it, sir . . . I'd like to think so—but I have a feeling we've not got to the bottom of it yet."

"What's worrying you?"

"I don't know," Dyson said. "I wish I did."

Nield grinned. "Hardly up to your usual standard!"

The telephone rang on the station sergeant's desk. "Call for you, sir, from Cambridge," the sergeant said.

Nield took the phone. "Yes . . .? *Really*. . . .? Well, that's very interesting. . . . Okay, tell them we'll be over right away." He hung up.

"Quite a morning we're having," he said. "They've found Gwenda Nicholls's suitcase at Cambridge railway station."

The station-master had the case in his office. There was no doubt about the identification. It had the letters G.L.N. in black beside the handle, and the remains of a Vistasund Hotel label on the end.

"Where was it found?" Nield asked.

"On a bench in the Ladies' Waiting Room," the station-master said. "I gather it's been there since the middle of the week—the cleaner didn't realise it had been abandoned until this morning. Then she took it to Lost Property and one of the chaps remembered the description."

"Good for him . . ." Nield opened the case. It contained a pale-blue jumper, a grey pleated skirt, a blue-flowered head scarf, an off-white woollen coat and a pair of navy-blue shoes.

He looked at Dyson. "Well, doesn't that just about settle it, Sergeant?"

Dyson's face was expressionless. "Does it, sir?"

"I'd say so . . . She knew the things she was wearing would identify her sooner or later—and the suitcase, too—so she changed in the Ladies' into other things she'd got with her, and cleared off. It all fits—and she's still alive."

"Where did she put her other belongings?"

"She could have bought a cheap case for those. Or made a bundle of them. No difficulty there . . ."

Dyson looked down at the clothes. "For a girl with less than ten pounds in her pocket," he said, "it seems a lot to abandon."

"Well, if she was determined to disappear, she didn't have much choice. She could hardly have left the case in the cloakroom—it might have been identified on the spot."

"Maybe it was Hunt who brought the case here," Dyson said. "To back up his story."

"Oh, come, Sergeant—if he'd killed the girl he wouldn't have kept a dangerous piece of evidence like her suitcase around for several days—he'd have got rid of it at once. Buried it, or something."

"H'm—I suppose so . . ."

"He certainly wouldn't have put it in the Ladies' Waiting Room, anyway. He'd have wanted to leave it as inconspicuously as possible—and for a man to put it in the Ladies' would have been a sure fire way of getting noticed. No one with a murder to hide would take a risk like that. . . ." Nield picked up the suitcase. "Okay—on our way."

"Where are we going, sir?"

"Ocken," Nield said. "I think it's time we put the suspect out of his misery."

Hunt was just emerging from the office as the police car drove up. He looked at Nield and the sergeant with unconcealed animosity. "Now what is it? Thumbscrews?"

"On the contrary," Nield said, "I've good news for you."

"Oh?"

"Two witnesses have come forward who say they saw your car parked in Peterborough on Saturday evening—just where you told us. They've identified you as the driver."

Hunt's face cleared a little. "Well, that's a bit of luck."

"It seems they were telephoning from the box close by. I'm surprised you didn't remember seeing them. A young couple . . ."

"I think I do vaguely remember them now," Hunt said. "I wasn't paying much attention at the time."

Nield gave an understanding nod. "That's not all, though—I've even better news. . . ." He produced Gwenda's case from the car. "I expect you recognise this."

Hunt stared at it. "Where did you get it?"

Nield told him of the Cambridge find. "It looks as though the girl *has* gone to ground somewhere."

"I never doubted it," Hunt said. He drew a long breath. "So what's the position now, Inspector?"

"The position, Mr. Hunt, is that I now accept your story—the whole of it—and that as far as you're concerned the case is over. I propose to notify the Press accordingly."

"Well, that's a relief," Hunt said. "Even if it *is* overdue . . . It hasn't been exactly pleasant for me these last few days."

"I realise that, Mr. Hunt—it's been on my mind quite a bit . . . I'm sorry about it—and I'll do all I can to repair the damage."

Hunt nodded, unsmiling. "Coming from the police, I suppose that ranks as a handsome apology. Forgive me if I'm not overwhelmed with gratitude. . . . Now, if you don't mind, I'd like to ring my fiancée . . ."

Back at headquarters, Nield reported to his superintendent on the latest turn of events, and afterwards told Dyson he could take the rest of the day off. He then drafted and dispatched a short statement for the Press, and telephoned Gwenda Nicholls's father at the Council offices in Peterborough. Since Gwenda's disappearance was now established as voluntary, he explained, the active police search would have to be called off—though of course if any information came in it would be passed on. He felt sure that Mr. and Mrs. Nicholls would be relieved that their worst fears had not been realised, and he hoped that Gwenda would in time return to them. Having relieved his conscience over Hunt, and done his best for the deprived parents, he relaxed.

Chapter Twelve

Dyson, at home in his mother's small, terrace house, was getting no pleasure from his afternoon of unexpected freedom. In, different circumstances he'd have been well content to spend a sunny hour or two in the pocket-handkerchief garden at the back, having fun with his baby daughter in her play-pen, giving the lawn a final autumn cut, tidying the borders. . . . But to-day, all he could do was brood. About himself—and about the case. . . .

He felt a little as though he'd been packed off home like a schoolboy in disgrace. Nield, he knew, hadn't meant it like that—Nield had simply felt he was overdue for some time off and had given it him at the first opportunity. But the fact remained that in the last stages of the case, the inspector had had no use for him—had found him, rather obviously, a bit of a trial. Nield had preferred to wind up the case on his own. . . .

Dyson found that humiliating. Rank was rank—but he knew his capacities. By now, if he hadn't let things slide after Mary's death, he might have been well on the way to being an inspector himself and handling his own cases. Of course, he'd no one but himself to blame—he wasn't complaining about that. He knew he'd made it clear that he'd lost his ambition, that he didn't really care. . . . But in this one case of Gwenda Nicholls, he'd have welcomed the chance to exercise a little authority.

In his view, Nield's final conclusions had been hasty, and his actions precipitate. Nield had been rattled by Henry Ainger—and he'd allowed himself to be unduly affected by concern for Hunt. Dyson felt no such concern. For another man in similar circumstances—perhaps. But not for Hunt. "I do not like thee,

Doctor Fell . . ." That, roughly, was the position.

It would have been pleasant, of course, to be able to believe that Nield was right, that Gwenda was alive . . . But Dyson distrusted the sudden, convenient accumulation of evidence that had faced them that day. There were aspects of the Peterborough identification—particularly the position of the parked car—that troubled him. And his doubts about the Cambridge find had grown rather than lessened. Several questions he hadn't thought of putting to Nield at the time had occurred to him since. Why, for instance, would Gwenda have waited three or four days before getting rid of her going-away outfit and that hot suitcase? Why would she have gone to a railway station to change?—she must have had a room somewhere, and it would have been easier to do it there. Why would she have risked carrying the case about in a crowded spot?—she'd have done better to leave it in a street at night. Or she could have hidden it somewhere—some place where she'd have had a chance to recover it later. And surely she'd have scraped off that tell-tale hotel label before going out with it. . . .? The incident wasn't right—it wasn't convincing. It was untidy . . . For that matter, there were loose, untidy ends everywhere. Dyson still hadn't got rid of his nagging feeling that he'd missed something important on his trip to Lingford. . . . A general dissatisfaction—that was what he felt about the case . . . But what use was a dissatisfaction that couldn't be given a precise reason or a shape? He'd have to come up with something better than that. . . .

Well, at least he had a little leisure now to think. . . . He began systematically going over all the evidence again in his mind. The whole case, from the anonymous letter onwards. Taking the points item by item. Questioning them. Particularly the odder items. . . . The only effect was to reinforce his suspicion of Hunt without producing anything new. The evening wore on, and he was still on the treadmill. No flash of illumination came to him; no vital clue suddenly stood out. But, around nine o'clock, something did occur to him that he hadn't thought of before. A small point of logic, it seemed at first—but the argument carried him on. . . . So much so that in the end he decided to risk a snub and phone Nield at his home.

"I'm sorry to bother you at this hour," he said, "but there's a point about the Hunt affair that I'd very much like to put to you—something we haven't discussed before . . . Could I come round and see you?"

"You want to reopen the case, eh?"

"It's never seemed closed to me, sir."

"H'm . . . Well, if you've got a new angle, Sergeant, of course I'd like to hear it . . . I'm on my own to-night. Drop in any time."

Dyson was there in less than ten minutes. Nield took him into the cosy back room he used as a private office. The inspector was wearing carpet slippers and an old cardigan, and smoking a curly, off-duty pipe. Two misted bottles of beer and two glasses stood on a tray. The omens looked good for friendly discussion.

"Well," Nield said, after he'd waved Dyson to a chair and poured the beer, "what's on your mind?"

"The anonymous letter," Dyson said.

"Oh, yes? What about it?"

Dyson leaned forward earnestly. "It's all a question of what we can reasonably accept, sir. . . . Now if that chap in the hide *had* seen Hunt in the fen with a girl, and heard a cry, and we'd followed the directions he gave and found a body—okay, the letter would be completely explained and there'd be no problem . . . But we found nothing—so we decided that that explanation was out."

Nield nodded. "We decided the letter writer was mistaken."

"Which would be perfectly all right," Dyson said, "if the letter had referred to some *other* night, and we'd found nothing . . . But it didn't—it referred to the night when Gwenda Nicholls disappeared."

Nield began to look interested. "Go on, Sergeant."

"So what we're being asked to believe," Dyson said, "is that some independent witness indicated Hunt as the possible murderer of a girl on a certain evening, *mistakenly*—but that on that very same evening Hunt *had* had a girl with him, a girl he had a strong motive for killing, who's since disappeared . . . Isn't that combination a bit too much of a coincidence to accept?"

Nield frowned. "Put like that, it sounds almost impossible . . . I can't think why it didn't strike me that way before." He sat silent for a while, contemplating the glowing bowl of his pipe. Dyson waited.

"Well, suppose we assume it *is* impossible," Nield said finally. "Where does it lead us?"

"If it's impossible," Dyson said, "one part of the combination must be wrong . . . Well, we know about Hunt and the girl—that's all established . . . So it's the independent witness we've got to look at again. If we can't accept that he was making an honest mistake, we've got to accept that he was lying . . . Maybe he wasn't so independent. Maybe he had a reason for writing what he did."

"You mean he might have been someone who had a grudge against Hunt—someone, who wanted to get him into trouble?"

"No, I don't think that," Dyson said. "Anyone hoping to get him into serious trouble through that letter would have had to know a lot. He'd have had to know that Hunt and Gwenda had met each other before, that she was at the site that day, that she was pregnant, and that Hunt had ambitious marriage plans which gave him a motive . . . I don't see how anyone could possibly have known so much—especially a local man who was also familiar with the fen . . . Except Hunt himself."

Nield glanced sharply at the sergeant. "Are you suggesting that Hunt wrote the letter?"

"That's what I wanted to put up to you," Dyson said. "To me, it seems the logical conclusion."

"It sounds pretty fantastic . . . *Why* would he have written it?"

"He could have been trying to mislead us," Dyson said. "Sending us to a place where he *hadn't* put the body—and mentioning the wrong time, a time when he was actually in Peterborough. Giving himself a sort of double alibi."

"But why bring it up at all, Sergeant . . .? If it hadn't been for the letter, there wouldn't have been anything to mislead us about. Hunt could have killed the girl and got rid of her body and simply kept quiet ... Her parents thought she was safely away on a job—they wouldn't have worried for a bit. The Bakers were no longer expecting her, so they wouldn't have said anything. It would have been quite a time before any inquiries started—and then the trail wouldn't have led to Hunt."

"It would if Gwenda had told someone she was going to see him," Dyson said.

"Well—we know she hadn't told her parents, or her girl friend."

"*We* know, sir—but did Hunt ...? Of course, she may have said she hadn't—but could Hunt have relied on that? He'd have known that girls in a jam usually confide in someone—and without necessarily admitting they've done so ... That wouldn't have been the only danger, either. Once the hue and cry had started, someone might have remembered seeing Gwenda in the village or even going into the site ... Could Hunt have been *sure* the trail wouldn't lead to him?"

"Not sure—no."

"Well, if he wasn't sure, mightn't he have decided it would be better to have an immediate inquiry, *with* an alibi, rather than risk a delayed inquiry without one?"

"That might explain sending *a* letter," Nield said, "but it wouldn't explain drawing attention to *himself* in it. He could have got his inquiry and his alibi without that. All he had to do was mention a man and a girl in the fen, and a scream, and give the time of the happening. We'd have made inquiries around the village;—and if we'd learned that a girl had gone to the site that day and hadn't been seen since, and we'd asked him about it, he could have told us his story about Gwenda and still have had his alibi for the time mentioned in the letter. If we hadn't learned about the girl—which is much more likely—he'd have had nothing to worry about."

Dyson gave a thoughtful nod.

"The fact is," Nield said, "if he did write that letter indicating himself, he was provoking a murder investigation that otherwise might never have happened and positively courting the worst sort of trouble for himself ... Why would any sane man do that?"

"I don't know, sir—unless he was anxious to get the whole thing over. Not have it hanging over his head . . . It seems pretty unlikely, I agree, but if that was the idea it's certainly worked. By provoking the inquiry, he's now in the clear with nothing on his mind."

"Sounds a bit like banging your head against the wall because it's nice when you stop," Nield said.

"Yes—it doesn't make much sense." Dyson was silent for a moment. "All the same, I can't help going back to where we began. Logic does suggest he wrote the letter—whatever his reason may have been . . . And there are other things that point the same way . . . Remember how at that first interview he didn't ask us how we got on to him? You said he wasn't given much of a chance—but he managed to ask quite a few other questions. I still think it was an odd oversight, if he didn't already know the answer . . . But if he'd sent us the letter that started everything, it was just the sort of slip he might have made."

"H'm. . . ."

"It would explain the anonymity, too," Dyson said. "I never did think much of the writer's excuse for not giving his name—that business about the girl friend . . . As a matter of fact, that whole business of the hide seems phoney to me now. If the chap had a girl with him, what was he doing looking out of the tower so much? The place might have been all right for a quick romp, but I can't see anyone just standing around there on a fine night."

Nield nodded slowly. "They're good points, Sergeant—I can see why you cling to your notion. But if we can't find a convincing reason . . ." He reached for his untouched glass of beer. "That suggestion of yours that Hunt wanted to mislead us—it falls down in other ways, you know. For instance—sending us to the wrong place. The final effect of that wasn't to mislead us—it was to make us doubt the letter's relevance to the case. Just the opposite of what he'd have wanted."

"True . . ."

"And if the intention was to mislead us about the time, Hunt would surely have covered himself better . . . It was pure chance that his visit to Peterborough was ever confirmed."

"I don't know about that," Dyson said. "He parked right under a lamp and next to a phone box. If he'd hoped to be seen and remembered, he couldn't have chosen a better place."

Nield looked doubtful. "It would have been a pretty casual attitude for a guilty man with so much at stake. Establishing his presence there would have been very important for him—not just because of the alibi, but because of his story about taking the girl back ..." Nield broke off. "And that's another thing ... Whatever Hunt's reason for being in Peterborough, we know he *was* there ... If his story wasn't true, and he hadn't taken the girl with him, where was she?"

"Dead and buried somewhere," Dyson said.

"No, Sergeant, that won't do ... She telephoned the Bakers' at half past seven—and Hunt must have left the site immediately after that or he wouldn't have been parked in Peterborough by nine-forty. He couldn't possibly have killed her, stowed her away safely, cleaned up the traces and himself—and still made it. He wouldn't even have had time to tie her up and gag her—not securely."

"I suppose not ..."

"So he must have taken her with him ... He'd hardly have left her alive and free at the site to be dealt with later."

Dyson frowned. *Alive and free at the site* ... The phrase held him. It chimed with something in his own mind. ... Suddenly his train of thought exploded in a riot of colour.

"Sir—I've got it ...! I knew I'd missed something ... The chrysanthemums!"

Nield looked at him strangely. "Chrysanthemums?"

"That bunch Hunt had on his car seat. He said they were for Susan Ainger. He was lying. They couldn't have been."

"Why not?"

"Not chrysanthemums. You didn't see the Aingers' garden—there are huge beds of them there. Every colour—a wonderful show ... He'd never have bought a bunch of chrysanthemums for her ... They must have been for Gwenda."

"For *Gwenda* ...? But that was on Monday afternoon—two days after she'd disappeared."

"If I'm right, about the flowers," Dyson said, "she hadn't

disappeared—she must have been around . . . Alive and free, as you said."

"But we were there, Sergeant—we went all over the place. There wasn't a sign of her."

"We didn't search the place, sir. She could have tucked herself away somewhere—voluntarily. She must have been playing along with Hunt if he was giving her flowers. . . ."

"But this is absurd," Nield said. "It would mean that Hunt told a lying story to explain a disappearance that hadn't happened, and allowed himself to be suspected of a murder that hadn't been committed. All with the girl still there . . ." His face suddenly tautened. "My God, you don't suppose . . .?" He looked at Dyson with startled eyes.

Dyson gazed back at him, no less startled. "That could be it, sir," he said. "That would explain everything. The letter to provoke an inquiry—Peterborough—all his behaviour—the suitcase still being around . . . And nothing else does."

Nield had already reached for his shoes.

"He didn't know he was in the clear until this afternoon, though," Dyson added. "And he wouldn't have done anything in daylight."

"Daylight was two hours ago," Nield said. "And once it was dark, why should he wait?" He grabbed his jacket. "Let's go. . . ."

They tore out to Dyson's car. Nield hurled himself into the passenger seat and slammed the door. "Give it all you've got, Sergeant."

He sat back as the car roared away. There were three big questions in his mind. Could such a fantastic idea really be true? If it was, would they be in time . . .? And how the devil had Hunt managed it. . . .?

PART THREE

Chapter One

The evening of that Saturday that Gwenda had come to the caravan site had been an anxious and exhausting one for Hunt. He'd had to re-think and perfect a plan that would guarantee safety as well as success—and he'd had to begin to put it into execution.

Immediately after their meal was over, he'd referred again to the importance of Gwenda not being seen. "I'm still a bit worried in case somebody notices you," he'd said. "Villagers are such dreadful gossips—and if the rumour gets around that I've got a girl living here with me, my boss is sure to hear about it."

Momentarily, Gwenda had looked troubled again.

"It's only that I don't want to be given the sack before I've landed a new job," Hunt had explained. "We're obviously going to need all the money we can get hold of from now on, for setting up house, so we must avoid a gap in my earnings if we can. Also, I'll need a reference from my present boss . . . It will pay us to take a little care."

"I do understand, Alan," Gwenda had said. "Tell me how I can help. You know I'll do anything you want me to."

"Well, the chief danger is that someone might come to the caravan and find you here . . . How would you feel about moving to one of the boats . . .? Me too, of course."

Gwenda had brightened at once. "*Could* we?"

"Why not . . .? There's a rather nice cruiser I'm supposed to be laying up for the winter—it's owned by a chap who's gone to America . . . It's the last one in the row, and right out of the way. Just the job for us."

"Wouldn't the owner mind?"

"No—he said I could use it if I wanted to . . . Come and have a look."

Hunt led the way to *Flavia*. Bushes at either end of the boat provided quite a bit of cover. "The ground's rather soft," he said. "Just a minute—I'll put something down . . ." He fetched a plank from the shed and laid it over the mud. "There—you'll be all right now, darling." He smiled at her. "Got to look after you in your condition, eh?"

Gwenda smiled back fondly. "You needn't worry about me. . . ." She stepped lightly into the cockpit. Hunt unlocked the cabin door and helped her down the short staircase. She gazed around, her eyes shining.

"It's lovely," she said. "A proper stove, and everything . . . Electric light—and a radio . . . And a fridge. . . .! Why, it's luxury."

"There's not a lot of space," Hunt said. "We can put everything in the van that we don't need, but it still won't be exactly roomy . . . You don't think we'll be too cramped?"

"I'm sure we won't. . . . And it'll be much more fun than the caravan." She began to explore—exclaiming at the little washroom, opening the hanging cupboard, the lockers and the drawers; admiring the galley with its cunningly-stowed crockery and its chromium taps, the smart gas fire, the softness of the two foam-rubber bunks. "I've never seen anything so neat and compact," she said. "It's like a doll's house."

"You won't feel lonely, will you, when you're on your own . . .? I'll have to be away quite a bit, you know, seeing clients. . . . As a matter of fact, I've got to see someone this evening about a sale—I may be away a couple of hours . . . Will you be all right?"

She laughed. "Of course I will. I'm not frightened of bogey men . . . I love it here."

"You'll have to draw the curtains over the windows when the lights are on—and not play the radio too loudly."

"I know . . . I'll be terribly careful."

Hunt gave a satisfied nod. "All right, then—I'll get your suitcase. And the bedclothes—I stripped them off this morning . . . I shan't be long."

footmarks—but its appearance was certainly sinister enough to arouse the interest of suspicious policemen . . . Yet everything would seem to have an innocent explanation, when nothing was found . . . A perfect job, in a perfect place . . .

He backed out carefully, checking all footmarks as he went, obliterating anything that looked at all identifiable. Near the drove he stopped and flattened some of the sedge at the edge of the track he'd made. No harm in giving the sleuths a little extra encouragement . . . Then he replaced the tools in the punt and walked quickly back to the dinghy. There was no sound from the site, no light except in the caravan. He re-crossed the lode, stripped off his muddy overalls and boots in the shed, returned to the van, and cleaned himself up.

Now for the letter he'd planned—the letter that would set off the inquiry. A plain sheet of paper, and a plain envelope. Or better still . . . He looked in his wallet. Yes, he still had a letter card. No chance of tracing a letter card. He began to write out his message—the message he'd already mentally drafted . . . Saying just enough to get things moving—yet couched in terms sufficiently vague to allow for an alternative explanation of the incident in the fen. Mentioning a time that would give him an alibi, if the Peterborough gamble came off. Directing the police to an untenanted grave, if they had the wit to work things out . . . A little masterpiece . . . Hunt felt immensely pleased with it. Pleased, too, that he'd thought of the hide, and of a way to exploit the lie of the land . . . And all without danger. Without a single really hazardous step having been taken . . .

He read the finished version through, satisfied himself that it said neither too much nor too little, and put it away in his wallet. For the moment, that was all. . . .

Gwenda stirred as he entered the boat. He touched her hair, said "Good-night, darling," and slipped into his bunk without turning on the light. He lay for a while, planning the next day's moves. Then he sank into the untroubled sleep of a man with nothing on his conscience.

In the morning he gave Gwenda a cup of tea in her bunk, cosseting her. Everything depended now on keeping her in a happy and contented frame of mind. Attentiveness, and a few kisses and caresses, should ensure that. He didn't think that she was wanting anything more at the moment—she was shy with him still, and showed no sign of making passionate advances. That suited him well ... In other circumstances, he'd have found her irresistible, lying only a few feet away from him with her lovely hair spread over the pillow and her blue eyes shining and her nightdress not all that opaque. He'd have been over there in a flash. But not now. He'd too much on his mind for sex. He was like a juggler, watching over half a dozen things at once ... And soon there'd be more of them ... At least, he thought, it was a stroke of luck that Susan was away for the week-end.

He washed and shaved, and then went off to the caravan to fetch eggs and bacon for breakfast. The village lay in a deep Sabbath silence, the fen was deserted. No danger threatened from anyone at the moment. But a fine October Sunday might well bring people out. He'd have to be careful. He stood for a while in thought, weighing a balance of risks. Gwenda was bound to get restive if he kept her a prisoner when the weather was good. It would be worth while accepting a few hazards to avoid that. He could probably work something out ... Maybe even kill two birds with one stone ...

Gwenda had dressed by the time he got back. At the sound of his approach she came out into the cockpit, smiling, and sniffing the air. She was still wearing the pleated skirt and blue jumper she'd had on the day before, but now her hair was pinned up on top of her head.

"That's sensible," he said. "Save you getting it caught in the floorboards!" He handed her the eggs and bacon. "It's going to be a lovely day again."

She nodded. "It seems a shame we can't go out ... It all looks so beautiful."

"Well, I've been thinking about that," Hunt said. "There's really no reason why you shouldn't go out by yourself ... You could take a walk in the fen."

Gwenda glanced across the lode. "How would I get there?"

"We could borrow a pram dinghy from one of the boats and keep it tied up on the outside of *Flavia* . . . Then, whenever you wanted to go off, you could row yourself over to the other bank."

"Oh, I'd love that."

"You'll have to make absolutely sure there's no one around before you set off—and before you row back."

"I will, darling—I'll be most careful."

"It might be as well to keep away from people, too—just to be on the safe side. Some folk are so nosy."

"I won't go near a soul."

"Good . . . And after dark we can go for a walk together, eh?"

"Yes, please," Gwenda said.

Hunt stood eyeing her. "You know, if you're going to mess about in boats and explore the fen, you really ought to have some old clothes . . . You'll ruin that nice jumper and skirt . . . Haven't you got anything?"

"I've got some slacks," Gwenda said, "but they're not old. I wasn't prepared for this sort of thing."

"No, of course not . . . I'll tell you what—I'll bring you some things from the store. I always keep a selection there for the boat people . . . How about a pair of jeans, a windcheater, a woolly cap and gum boots . . .? That's mostly what the students wear when they come grubbing about in the fen. Then if you catch on a bramble or fall in a pool, it won't matter."

Gwenda smiled. "All right, darling . . . I'm in your hands."

"You'd be in my arms," Hunt said, "if you weren't holding bacon and eggs . . . Okay, I'll get the things while you cook breakfast." He went off, whistling.

He was back in a few minutes, rowing along the lode in a tiny green-painted dinghy that he'd taken from a nearby boat top. He made it fast to *Flavia* and climbed aboard with an armful of clothes.

"There you are," he said. "Service. . . ."

"I'll try them on after breakfast," Gwenda said.

The blue jeans and the gumboots fitted perfectly. So did the T-shirt Hunt had brought with him. The woolly cap had a blue band round it that matched the jeans. The brown windcheater was a shade on the large side, but Gwenda said it would do. She seemed pleased with the outfit.

"We're going to be a bit short of locker space with all these extra things," Hunt said. "Why not put your good outfit in the suitcase and let me take it to the caravan? That'll make more room in the forepeak, too. We don't want to get cluttered up."

"All right," Gwenda said.

Hunt grinned. "I suppose you think I'm bossy."

"You are, a bit."

"I'm sorry . . . It's all well meant, darling."

"I know," Gwenda said. "Anyway, I don't seem to mind being bossed by you."

The morning passed very smoothly. Gwenda slipped across the lode just before eleven, rowing a short distance downstream first and tying up to the bush on the opposite bank that Hunt had pointed out to her. Hunt watched her for a while from the van window as she strolled along Stoker's Drove, lingered in the sun, stopped to examine something that had caught her eye . . . It was a good thing, he thought, that she was so fond of the country—some girls would have hated wandering in the fen alone, but she was obviously revelling in it. . . . As for the change of clothes, he was delighted. The new outfit provided the perfect disguise—especially with her hair tucked away under the cap. No one seeing her now would connect her for a moment with the girl who'd arrived the day before. . . .

While she was away, he strolled into the village and posted his letter card.

Approvingly, he noted her cautious return around midday—her seemingly casual approach to the bank, her careful inspection of the lode and the site before she rowed across. She was obviously entering into the spirit of the thing—regarding it all as a bit of an adventure . . . And it seemed that she'd had a wonderful morning. All the time she was preparing lunch, she chatted gaily about the fen and the interesting things she'd found there.

After lunch, Hunt faced a new problem—though one he'd already foreseen.

"I think," Gwenda said, looking slightly worried, "I ought to send a line to Mum and Dad. They'll be expecting a letter . . ."

"I suppose so."

"The thing is, what am I going to say?"

"If I were you," Hunt said, "I'd settle for a postcard at the moment, and keep it vague . . . Just say everything's fine, and you're enjoying yourself, and you'll be writing again soon . . . That'll keep them happy—and in a few days, we'll probably be able to go and see them."

"But they'll wonder why it doesn't come from St. Neots."

"That's true. . . ." Hunt appeared to consider. "Look, I really ought to pop over to Cambridge this afternoon—and St. Neots isn't much farther on . . . I could post it for you."

"That's a good idea . . . What are you going to do in Cambridge?"

"There's a big garage there that's open on Sunday—it's run by a man named Joe Crawford whom I used to know in Brighton. He's got a big sales department and I think he might give me a decent job. . . . Anyway, it's a chance—don't you agree?"

"Oh, yes," Gwenda said quickly.

"If it came off, I could tell my boss I was leaving and get a testimonial from him and we might be away in a few days. . . . Cambridge wouldn't be a bad place to live, either. Have you ever been there?"

"No. . . ."

"I'm sure you'd like it. It's a very lively city, because of all the undergraduates milling around; and of course the colleges are beautiful and there are nice walks along the Cam . . . Just the place to stroll with a pram . . . And there are quite a lot of new houses on the outskirts. We could borrow some money from a building society."

"You have to put something down," Gwenda said.

Hunt smiled. "I'll let you into a little secret, my love—I've saved up a bit . . . Not much, but enough for that."

"It's a nice secret," Gwenda said. "Have you got any more?"

"A few," Hunt said. "You'll know about them all in time . . . Now what about writing that postcard while I do the washing up?"

In the afternoon he drove a few miles out of the village, parked in a field gateway, tore up the postcard and threw the pieces into a ditch. Then, for a little over an hour, he sat and read the Sunday papers. Having used up the necessary amount of time, he returned to the caravan site.

Gwenda was resting in the boat when he got back. "Did you have any luck?" she asked.

"Yes, I think there's quite a good chance," Hunt, said cheerfully. "Crawford's looking into the possibilities —I'll be seeing him again in a day or two . . . Anyway, I've got several more ideas if that one falls through. Trust me!"

"I do," Gwenda said. "Did you post my card?"

"Yes, at St. Neots . . . Now everything's taken care of."

"Do you write much to your own mother?" Gwenda asked.

For a second, Hunt was caught off balance. He was about to say that his mother was dead—then he remembered that in Norway he'd told Gwenda he was writing to her. A near thing. . . .!

"Oh, I write about once a fortnight," he said; "She likes to hear from me fairly often—she's a widow, and she finds life a bit lonely. She'll be tickled to death when I tell her about you. . . . That's one of the first things I want you to do—meet her."

"I shall love to, Alan . . . Where does she live?"

"Near Salisbury," Hunt said. "She's got a little cottage—you'll like it. Roses round the windows, and all that . . ." He turned nonchalantly away, glanced at the barometer, gave it a tap. "Steady as a rock . . . We'll have a nice moonlight walk after supper."

The moonlight walk was a little more taxing than Hunt had expected. As they strolled through the fen, arms twined round each other and heads close together, Gwenda said, "What's Lesley like, darling?"

For a blank moment, Hunt couldn't think who Lesley was . . . Then he remembered. Susan, of course . . . "Oh," he said, "She's tall—slim—quite a nice face."

"Is she pretty?"

"No, not really . . . She's jolly."

"I expect she's clever."

"Not particularly . . . Just ordinary."

Gwenda laughed. "I bet you say that about all the girls. . . . Did she meet your mother?"

"Good gracious, no. It hadn't reached that stage."

"Did you tell your mother about her?"

"No, I didn't, as a matter of fact. Perhaps I had a feeling it wouldn't come to anything. . . . Why this sudden interest?"

"I just wondered about her . . . When did you say she was coming back, darling?"

"It should be about next Sunday. She's on a small cargo boat in the Mediterranean, so the date isn't quite certain."

"I suppose her father's well off?"

"He must be—he owns Cosy Caravans and it's quite a big company. I don't much like him, actually—he's very curt and short-tempered. I'll be glad to get away from him."

There was a little pause. Then Gwenda said, "Lesley won't be coming here, will she?"

"Oh, no—I'll go and see *her* directly I hear she's back. You needn't worry—I won't let anything embarrassing happen. Just leave it all to me—I'll fix it. . . . Anyway, we may not be here by then."

"You're sure you won't be sorry about her?"

"Of course not, my sweet . . . I told you—it never amounted to anything much."

"I expect I'm silly," Gwenda said. "I won't ask you any more questions."

"I don't mind. . . ." Hunt released himself, and gently dabbed his forehead with his handkerchief. The night had begun to feel quite warm.

Monday was the crucial day—the day the letter card would reach the police, the day they were pretty sure to come. Hunt had prepared for it with meticulous care, going over every detail of the story he would tell, trying to foresee the likely order of events. He expected a police car and plain-clothes men, rather than P.C. Blake. Probably they'd come in the morning. He must show mild surprise at seeing them. If they produced the letter, he must be astonished and indignant. If, as seemed more likely, they preferred to probe first, he must be forthcoming about Gwenda's visit. He must tell his story in a straightforward, natural way, taking acceptance for granted. The chances were that they would then leave. They'd hardly bother to look around the place until they'd checked whether Gwenda was in Peterborough. All the same, it would be a time of exceptional risk. A time when Gwenda must on no account be seen. . . .

"I'm expecting some trade customers to-day, darling," he told her over breakfast. "Friends of the boss—rather tricky . . . Do you feel like lying low, or will you go for a walk?"

"Oh, I'll go into the fen," Gwenda said. "I've found a a nice grassy spot next to a pool—I'll lie there and sunbathe."

"Good—then I should make an early start. . . . And be specially careful how you come back to-day, won't you? If you see anyone around, stay on the other side of the lode till they've gone. Okay. . . .?"

"Yes, darling."

"You can take the newspaper—I'll be too busy to read it. I've got to get through some letters before the customer come . . . See you around lunch-time."

He strolled along to the office, made a couple of business calls, and then settled down to his papers. He felt slightly keyed up, but very confident. About eleven, he heard a car approaching. He glanced through the window. A car with a police sign over the roof. He went out, looking mildly surprised. . . .

Gwenda lay beside the pool, her head pillowed on her folded windcheater, her chin tilted so that the sun shone full on her face, her eyes closed. Enjoying the scents and sounds of the fen. Basking . . . But also thinking . . .

Thinking about the baby she was going to have. Hers and Alan's.

It was a delicious thought—now. With a little smile playing about her lips, she marvelled at the change that these last few days had brought. She had been so abysmally wretched, so alone and friendless. And now she was so happy. She was in love with Alan—and she was sure he was in love with her. He showed it all the time. He was so tender, so considerate and kind ... And so reassuring, too, in his confidence. A man she felt she could rely on. ... Of course, she didn't know him very well—but she soon would. Once they were married. ...

It would be marvellous, she thought, when she could tell someone about it. No doubt Alan was quite right to want to keep everything secret for a few days, and she didn't really mind going off on her own—in fact, she was having a wonderful holiday. But she didn't much care for secrecy—she'd really hated deceiving her parents. It was one thing to feel independent and want to leave home, and quite another to be cut off by the lies you'd told. ...

Still, it wouldn't last much longer. ...

So that was the first hurdle taken, Hunt thought, as he watched the two policemen drive away. ... He felt very satisfied with the show he'd put on. He'd been cool, candid, completely master of the situation. And they'd believed his story. He'd impressed them. They'd probably thought he was rather a decent fellow. ... But the real test was still ahead. About three hours ahead, Hunt guessed. Just long enough for the two-way journey to Peterborough and a few inquiries there. They'd be back like a shot when they found Gwenda hadn't come home. This time, brandishing the letter ... The second hurdle was going to be a lot higher than the first. ...

It was just before one o'clock when Gwenda returned to the site—so inconspicuously that Hunt himself didn't know she was around until he heard her dinghy bump against *Flavia's* hull. She climbed quickly aboard, with a conspiratorial smile. Hunt remembered to kiss her. Kissing her was like an entrance fee for the next lap. ...

"I believe you've caught the sun," he said.

"I know. . . . It was almost *too* hot out there—but lovely . . ." She got herself a drink of squash and flopped on the cabin seat. "Did you have a good morning?"

"Yes, everything went very well," Hunt said. "I'm afraid the men are coming back this afternoon, though—they're interested in the Midget vans and want to go over one with a fine comb. . . . I'm sorry about this, darling—it must be an awful bore for you, having to keep clearing off—and I'm sure you're tired. . . . Shall we not bother about it any more—just risk the boss finding out about you . . . Money isn't every thing. . . ."

"Oh, no, Alan, we mustn't do that—not just to save a little trouble. . . . Perhaps I needn't go so far this time?"

"I should think it would be all right if you just popped over the lode," Hunt said. "*I* know—I'll give you my camera to sling over your shoulder, and a notebook, and you can sit in the shade somewhere and pretend you're studying nature. . . . Then I'll give you a shout when the coast's clear. How about that?"

"Yes, that's better. . . ." Gwenda looked relieved. "Did you get the bread and extra milk, darling?"

"No, I didn't have time. . . . I'll dash into the village after lunch—the customers won't be back for a little while."

"I hate you having to bother with the shopping," Gwenda said. "I feel it's my job now." Hunt grinned. "You'll have plenty of it later, sweetie. Make the most of your leisure while you can."

"You're spoiling me," Gwenda said.

He saw her safely across the lode at two o'clock. As soon as she'd gone, he set to work to remove the more obvious signs of her sojourn at the site. There was no need, he decided, for extreme precautions—merely for ordinary care.

First, *Flavia*. . . . Hunt emptied the drawers and lockers that Gwenda had been using, put her things in an orderly pile between sheets of newspaper, and hid them away in the forepeak under a coil of rope. In the galley, he stowed away the cooking utensils. In the cabin, he rolled up the bedding, pulled out the bunk cushions and up-ended them, took out some floorboards. . . . To the casual eye, the boat really did look now as though it was being cleared out for the winter. . . .

Second, Gwenda's suitcase. . . . A thorough search would lead to its discovery wherever it was, of course—but anything short of that shouldn't be dangerous. . . . Hunt slid it under the tarpaulin cover of one of the cruisers. . . .

Third, footprints. . . . It didn't matter that the marks of Gwenda's shoes should be around the site, since she was known to have visited the place. But a concentration of female gumboot marks around *Flavia* might not be a good thing. . . . Hunt did a quick job of obliteration at the approaches. . . . ,

He still had time, he reckoned, to do his shopping before the police returned. He drove into the village and bought the food supplies he needed and a large bunch of chrysanthemums for Gwenda—which he'd say were for Susan if anyone asked. A pleasantly impudent touch, that—it appealed to him. . . . Then, at the T-junction on the way back, he narrowly avoided hitting a lorry. As he braked and swerved, he caught sight of the approaching police car. He guessed they'd noticed him. A close thing—and not good for his image. He wondered if they'd say anything about it—but, with murder on their minds, they didn't . . .

The interview was tough—but never for a moment out of Hunt's control. It had been easy to foresee the questions—and it was easy now to produce the planned explanation and reactions. To account for the fact that he hadn't seen Gwenda to her door. To show astonishment at the suggestion of murder—the more convincingly, since he knew that she was alive. To resent the letter, and the police suspicions. To show anger when it seemed that his future would be threatened . . . But, above all, to build up his motive and his opportunity. To seize the moment for disclosing that he had a fiancée. To demonstrate how keen he'd been to marry her. To make sure the police were handed every scrap of evidence against him—so that, if they eventually admitted error, it would be the strongest possible case they had rejected. . . .

The walk round the site with them afterwards had its tensions. Not because of Gwenda, whom he could see fifty yards downstream apparently sketching something in the reeds and looking exactly like a young field worker. It was when the hostile police sergeant put his head inside *Flavia* that Hunt momentarily held his breath. Any close inspection would produce evidence of recent double occupation. . . . But the slight danger quickly passed, as he'd guessed it would. The disorder had an authentic look. Besides, the very last thing the police could be thinking at that moment was that Gwenda might still be at the site. From their point of view, she was either dead and buried in the fen, as the letter had suggested, or hiding away in some place of her own. . . .

All the same, he felt relieved when they'd gone. The afternoon had been quite a strain. No one could say he was earning his prospective fortune easily. . . .

As soon as the police were well clear of the site he made the boat ship-shape again, put Gwenda's belongings back in the locker and drawers in the order in which he'd taken them out, and returned the suitcase to the caravan. He waited till an angler along the lode had decided to call it a day, and a picnicking couple had departed, and then signalled to Gwenda that it was safe to cross.

"They bought four Midgets," he told her jubilantly, as she joined him. "Enough commission to buy us a three-piece. . . ."

The pattern of his juggling act took on a new complexity that evening. Susan was due back from London and would expect attention. While Gwenda prepared supper, Hunt slipped along to his office and telephoned her.

"Hallo, my sweet," he said. "It's been such a long week-end without you. . . . How did the trip go?"

"Very well, darling. . . ."

"Was the Excelsior comfortable?"

"Oh, yes. . . ."

"And you saw the Cromptons?"

"Yes . . ."

"What about the shopping?"

"Well, we didn't get as much done as we hoped—but I've got a perfectly marvellous dress. . . ."

"Good . . . When can I see it?"

"Oh, not yet—it's being altered . . . But I've got some other things to show you. Can you come over this evening?"

"I don't think I can, darling—I'm supposed to be seeing a bloke. . . . What about to-morrow?"

"Yes, all right. . . ." There was a pause, the sound of voices at Susan's end. "Mummy says come and have dinner with us."

"Fine—it's a date. . . . Who else did you see yesterday. . . .?"

They chatted for several minutes, exchanging news and the usual sweet nothings. Then, with a loud kiss into the telephone, Hunt rang off.

That was all right, he thought. He wouldn't be able to keep the date—but his unfolding plan would take care of that. . . . Now back to Gwenda. . . .

He was a bit perturbed to see the thick mist over the fen on Tuesday morning—a break in the weather would make it much more difficult to keep Gwenda contented during his necessary absences. But the forecast was reassuring, and presently the sun began to peep through.

They had a quiet morning—Gwenda happily doing the chores in the boat, "playing at houses," as Hunt teasingly said—while he retired to the caravan to "work" and watch for anyone approaching the site. From the window, he kept a close eye on the fen and the lifting mist. He wasn't at all surprised when, shortly after midday, he saw through his binoculars the police sergeant enter Stoker's Drove and the inspector join him soon afterwards. It was the obvious next move. Well, he wished them joy of their digging. . . .

He lunched with Gwenda in the boat, in an atmosphere brightened by the glow of chrysanthemums. Over the meal, he talked cheerfully of his job prospects. He'd spoken to Crawford again on the telephone that morning, he said—and it now seemed to be a question mainly of salary. He might have to drop a little in basic pay if he took the job, but it would only be for a short time, and he was good at selling cars. He'd have to pop over to Cambridge again that evening, he said—but he wouldn't be away any longer than he could help. . . .

In the early afternoon, while Gwenda strolled along the bank of the lode, he considered the moves ahead. The police, having found nothing in the fen, would presumably begin to search for the missing girl around the country. That meant that to-morrow, or the next day, the story would break in the Press. . . . To-night, for safety, he'd better do something about the radio in the boat—say it had gone wrong, and take it away for repair. . . . And there must be no, more newspapers for Gwenda after to-morrow—he'd have to think of some explanation to cover that. . . . Fortunately she hadn't appeared to be an avid newspaper reader—she preferred magazines and books. And he'd still plenty of those in the caravan. . . .

In a day or two now, he thought, he should be able to judge how things were going. If they went wrong, he'd have no alternative but to clear out. Even with his powers of invention, he couldn't hope to talk himself out of what he'd said and done—either with the police, or with Gwenda. But he had his passport, and enough money to get by. And what he'd done so far certainly wasn't extraditable. He doubted if the police would even be able to put a name to it . . . It would be a financial catastrophe, of course—but no worse than if he'd done nothing at all. He'd have lost Susan anyway. . . . Meanwhile, the big prize still glittered. . . .

The latter part of Tuesday afternoon, and the evening, were exceptionally busy.

While Gwenda was still out on her walk, Hunt took her suitcase from the caravan wardrobe and put it with a light raincoat in the boot of his car.

At five o'clock he telephoned Susan, cancelled his dinner date, and arranged to meet her instead at Hayes Corner.

At five-thirty Gwenda returned, and during the short time he had to spare Hunt went out of his way to be specially charming to her. It was a wrench, he said, to leave her again—but this time he hoped to bring back really good news from Cambridge. He kissed her, and she wished him luck.

He reached Hayes Corner a little after six and told Susan of the "jam" he was in. It was a wearing interview—but with precisely the result he'd foreseen. A strong-minded, loyal girl like Susan would never have thought of not standing by him in his hour of need. . . .

From Hayes Corner, he drove fast to Cambridge railway station. Concealing most of the case under the raincoat slung over his arm, he walked briskly into the station. His intention had been to leave the case in the General Waiting Room—the best he could hope to achieve. Then, as he passed the Ladies' Waiting Room, he noticed two girls sauntering across the concourse towards the door. They were smart, foreign. . . . Talking volubly in French. . . . As they passed Hunt, he saw that their luggage was labelled Paris. Obviously going home . . . He addressed them—courteous, smiling—and in bad French, which amused them. Would they oblige him by taking his wife's case into the Ladies' Waiting Room and putting it on a seat? They didn't ask why. They simply smiled, and took it. It was as easy as that. . . . Hunt went back to the car. The whole episode had lasted only a few seconds. . . .

It was a bit of a gamble, of course. He knew that. If Gwenda suddenly insisted on having the case, he'd be in a spot. But he didn't think she would—he could see no reason why she should . . . Anyway, the whole plot was a gamble—with acceptable risks. . . . Gwenda, after all, was still alive. . . .

He got back to the site in time for a late supper. "Well," he announced cheerfully, as he entered the cabin, "I think the job's in the bag, darling . . . I've brought a bottle of wine from the van—let's celebrate."

Wednesday was peaceful, like the eye of a hurricane. In the world outside, the search must by now have started—but at the site there wasn't a ripple. Hunt looked carefully through the morning paper, the *Record*, found it harmless, and passed it on to Gwenda. Having quietly removed the battery from the radio, he reported that it was out of order and that he'd have to get it seen to. He took it to his office, and put the battery back in again. While he was there, he rang Susan, as he'd promised.

For Gwenda, it was the most domestic day they'd yet had. Hunt had no appointments outside the site, and the two genuine customers who called didn't keep him long. He was in and around the boat a good deal, making up for his earlier absences and those to come, keeping Gwenda happy. Now that he was supposedly waiting only for a final word from Crawford, there was more talk of plans, of the kind of house they might get, of the sort of furniture they liked. . . . Sickening talk, Hunt found it—but no one would have guessed as much from his enthusiastic manner. . . .

At six o'clock, listening surreptitiously to the news bulletin in his office, he heard the first mention of the missing girl. The story was about to break.

After the news, he had a second quick talk with Susan on the telephone.

Thursday brought the first news in the papers and the first reference to Hunt—an innocuous mention in the *Record*. Hunt destroyed the paper, and went to prepare Gwenda for the invasion he knew must follow.

"I'm afraid I'm going to have a shockingly busy day to-day," he told her. "Customers calling, appointments to go and see people—it's extraordinary at this time of year . . . A bit ironic, too, when I'm just on the point of packing it all in. . . . I'm afraid it'll mean another outing for you."

Gwenda looked a bit downcast for a moment—but she soon recovered. "Never mind, darling," she said. "Won't it mean extra commission?"

"Oh, it'll mean that, all right. . . . But I really hate sending you off."

She smiled. "I'm all right, Alan, really. . . . I do like the fen very much, and it's still nice weather, and after all I won't be seeing very much more of it, will I?"

He kissed her. "I love you so much."

"Anyway," she said, "you'll be out working every day when we're married, so what's the difference. . . . I don't expect to keep you in my pocket all the time."

"You're very understanding, darling."

"I'll take a book and a picnic," she said. "There are a lot of paths I haven't explored yet."

Hunt nodded. "You needn't stay in the fen if you don't want to—you could strike off across the fields. . . . But don't lose your way. And no talking to any strange men!"

"I wouldn't dream of it," Gwenda said, smiling. "Once is enough!"

It was an enormous relief to Hunt when she'd gone. Now the day was his. Perhaps the most vital day of all.

It proved as busy as he'd expected. From ten o'clock onwards, the phone in the office rang incessantly. Soon, reporters began to arrive—sceptical men, with searching questions. Hunt gave them better copy than they'd dreamed of. A human story, and a splendid mystery. A volunteered set of facts that seemed to damn him. A motive as well as an opportunity. They must have it all, and make the worst of it. That was the plan. . . .

In the mid-morning, Hunt rang Susan at the Crown, and told her how things were developing. Her father, he learned, had gone to London. Well, he said, she'd better try to get in touch with him and tell him there was trouble. He would read about it in the evening papers, anyway—they couldn't keep it to themselves any longer. Things had moved unexpectedly fast. Obviously, they'd all have to meet. . . .

A crescendo of activity now. A call back from Susan. Her father on his way home. A family conclave fixed at the Aingers' house. More reporters. One or two local people dropping in. An anxious telephone call to Nield asking if there was any news of Gwenda. Must keep up the front. . . . No sign of Gwenda as the time for the conclave approached. Hunt scribbled a note for her before he left. "Back as soon as I can—not sure when. Keep your head down!" He'd no choice now but to trust to her discretion. . . .

The climax at Copper Beeches. . . . Perhaps the most difficult confrontation of all—but Hunt felt he could face it with confidence. His story, by now, had been thoroughly tried and tested, and no one had found any flaw in it. Susan was already won over, and he could rely on her unwavering support. As for Ainger, he might be shrewd in business but he wasn't all that smart about people or he'd have rumbled his prospective son-in-law long ago. And he certainly wouldn't want to believe Hunt a murderer. Neither would Mrs. Ainger. So it should be all right. Most people believed what they wanted to believe. Like Gwenda. . . .

The family were in the sitting-room when Hunt arrived. He greeted them in a quietly normal way, kissing Mrs. Ainger, waving to Susan, saying "Hallo, sir," to Ainger with just the right touch of deference.

Ainger had the look of a man holding himself in with difficulty. "Well, this is a fine state of affairs, Alan . . . Have you seen what they're saying?" He thrust the London evening papers into Hunt's hand.

"No," Hunt said, "but I can guess." He glanced at the headlines, made a wry face over them—then turned apologetically to Ainger. "I'm sorry you had to find out this way, sir. . . . Susan's probably told you—we were hoping the girl would be found right away, and that you and Mrs. Ainger needn't be worried by it. Otherwise, I meant to tell you myself—but things moved too fast."

"I wish to God you had told me," Ainger said. "I'd have advised you not to talk to reporters."

"They were very pressing," Hunt said. "It was almost impossible not to . . . I wouldn't have brought Susan and the family into it, of course, but one of the chaps had already found out about my engagement, in the village. . . . As for the girl, when they asked me who she was and what she was doing at the site, it seemed only sensible to tell them. It's not as though I had anything to hide."

"That's right," Susan said. "It was much better to tell the truth."

Ainger grunted. "Well, the damage is done now, anyway . . . All right—let's have the full story. . . ."

Once more, Hunt told his tale. Simply, and with dignity. Ainger heard him out in simmering silence. When it was over, he began to fire questions. Their drift was reassuring. Ainger wasn't suspicious, Hunt realised—he was furious. Not with Hunt, but with the police and the newspapers. He was asking questions to gather ammunition. It was more than an hour before the exhausting thrash over the details came to an end—and by then, Hunt had won a powerful ally.

"Well," Ainger said, "I think you've been treated abominably."

"It certainly hasn't been pleasant," Hunt said. "What I regret most, of course, is that you've all been brought into it. I expect Susan told you I offered . . ."

Susan broke in. "Now don't start that again, darling, please."

Ainger said, "Mrs. Ainger and I appreciated your motives, Alan—it was a proper gesture. . . . But of course Susan wouldn't hear of it. She's a fighter, and so am I—and I'm sure you are . . . To-morrow we'll go along together and see my solicitor."

Hunt appeared to consider that. "I think it's premature," he said after a moment—knowing very well that he'd have no time to see anyone during the next few days. "Frankly, I can't take this stuff in the papers seriously—and I certainly don't feel I need defending. . . . I'm sure the girl will be found very soon, and then the whole thing will fizzle out."

"Suppose she isn't found?"

"Then we'll have to think again—but let's give it a day or two. . . . At the moment, I don't see what a solicitor could do."

"He could make trouble," Ainger said . . .

"I dare say. . . . All the same, I'd sooner wait."

"Well, you must do as you like," Ainger said. "*I'm* certainly going to make trouble. . . . What's the name of the fellow in charge of the case?"

Back to Gwenda now for the tail-end of the evening. Invented stories about the day's hectic business. Mechanical expressions of affection, inquiries about her picnic and her walk. The telephone still ringing. Sudden dashes from the boat to answer it. . . . All the time, too, Hunt had to watch for car lights, to listen for footsteps, to be ready to intercept the police if they returned, or any other visitor . . . He found it hard, now, to give Gwenda even minimum attention. . . .

Friday . . . More telephoning, while Gwenda did the morning chores. An early call to Susan . . . A call from Ainger, with an account of his visit to the police. Confidence and encouragement exchanged—but more talk of solicitors . . . A call from the manager of Cosy Caravans, angry about the publicity, demanding explanations. . . . Back in the boat, no peace either . . . Gwenda, for the first time, a bit restive—asking if Hunt had rung Crawford and what was happening. Hunt saying he had; pretending he was writing to his boss that day to give his notice and ask for the testimonial Crawford wanted—then the deal should be clinched. . . . Stalling—for the sixth day . . . This couldn't go on much longer. None of it. Hunt knew only too well that he'd built a house of cards. Soon, something would topple it. He couldn't go on handling Gwenda, and Susan, and Ainger, and the police, and the Press, and his firm. The situation was almost out of hand. . . . He wished now that he *had* gone into a pub in Peterborough and established his alibi. He'd underrated the mounting pressure of events, overrated the time he could hold out . . . What the devil had happened about that suitcase? Surely someone had found it by now . . .

Then, as he sat in his office, fingering his passport, the police car came again. Nield with his absolution. . . . Peterborough confirmed, *and* the suitcase found . . . Easy, now, for Hunt to play his penultimate act with cold dignity. "If you don't mind, I'd like to ring my fiancée . . ." The brief, ecstatic talk to Susan. The message for her parents. The relief as the storm subsided. . . . It had been a near thing—but the plan had worked . . .

Gwenda was curious when he returned to the boat. "Wasn't that a police car?" she asked.

"Yes," Hunt said. "Some fellow's passed us a dud cheque—very annoying. But they think they'll get him . . . Gosh, I feel quite tired."

He lay on his bunk, as the day drew to its close, thinking.

The gamble had paid off. He'd exposed himself to the strongest suspicions. By his letter, and his story, and Gwenda's disappearance, he'd built the most powerful case against himself that anyone could build. No worse evidence could be brought against him. And he'd been exonerated. He was officially cleared of the crime he hadn't committed.

Now he could safely commit it.

Nothing could be done before dark—but after that, the sooner the better. The empty fen would be as safe to operate in at nine o'clock as at twelve. And every extra moment at the site was a moment of hazard.

Hunt could hardly wait now for dusk to fall. The strain of facing Gwenda, of cosily chatting in these last few hours of her life, had become unbearable. The supper she offered him was more than he could stomach, and he had to make excuses. For an hour before dark he prowled alone around the site, nervously eyeing the entrance, broodingly eyeing the fen. Watching the light fade. . . .

At eight o'clock he went back to the boat. Gwenda was sitting with her elbows on the cabin table, looking thoughtful.

"Darling," she said, "when are we going to see Mum and Dad?"

Hunt fought down his sudden, overwhelming irritation. It was vital that he stayed on good terms with her to the end. Watch it, boy, he told himself. Keep calm. Don't spoil everything now. . . .

"I don't know," he said. "When do you want to?"

"Well, I've been thinking—there's no reason why we shouldn't go quite soon, is there? I mean, your new job's fixed, so there's nothing to wait for."

"That's true."

"I *would* like to get it over, Alan . . . And anyway, I'd like to see them again. I was wondering what's the best thing to do. Should I go on my own first and break it to Mum. . . .? What do you think?"

"It's up to you," Hunt said.

"Of course, I could tell her everything in a letter—but that seems a bit cowardly . . . I think perhaps we'd better go together—they'll feel better about things when they actually see you. . . . What about going on Monday?"

"Yes, Monday would be all right."

"We could drive over and get there after tea, when Dad comes home."

Hunt gave a curt nod.

"I'll have to let them know I'm coming. If I write now they'll be sure to get the letter on Monday morning. . . . Could you let me have some paper and an envelope?"

"Why not do it later?" Hunt said. "I was just thinking it would be nice to go for a row. It's a lovely night, and the moon'll be up before long."

"I'd sooner do it now," Gwenda said. "It's been a bit on my mind. . . . Then we'll go for a row. I'd like to."

"Very well. . . ." Seething, Hunt went to the van and got a pad and envelopes. She'd been so amenable all these days—why the hell did she have to get obstinate now? Of course, he could finish her off right there in the boat, and shut her up. But then there'd be the business of moving the body. It would be much easier if he could get her to go into the fen under her own steam. And safer. Better to wait. . . .

He returned quickly with the writing things. "Here you are. . . ."

"I think I'll just say I'm bringing someone with me," Gwenda said. "It might help to prepare them."

He nodded. "Don't be too long, that's all . . ." He went out, and started prowling again. Watching the car lights sweeping through the village. Watching apprehensively in case one of them turned into the site. He'd arranged with Susan to see her to-morrow—but suppose she took it into her head to drive over to-night after all. . . .?

Every few minutes he looked into the cabin to see how Gwenda was getting on. Slowly, it seemed . . . She appeared to be in the throes of a difficult composition. "Don't hurry me, darling," she said. *Hurry* her . . . ! He'd lost a valuable hour already . . . It could all have been over by now . . .

Gwenda had made several false starts. Finally she wrote:

Dear Mum and Dad,

I expect you'll be surprised to hear that I'm thinking of coming to see you quite soon. All sorts of things have been happening since I left—quite nice ones, really, but not at all what you suppose. I didn't go to the Bakers' after all—something happened, and I've been in a different place, a lovely spot not far from Newmarket ... I want to tell you all about it, Mum—about what I've been doing, I mean. Would it be all right if I came home late on Monday afternoon, so I could see you and Dad together? And perhaps stay for a day or two? You won't be able to answer this, so I'll take it I can come, because it's rather important. I'll be bringing someone with me, a man that you've met. I'm going to be married, Mum, and everything's going to be all right. I'm happy—very happy, really—but it will be a relief to see you and tell you everything. All my love to Dad and you until we meet. ...

Gwenda read it through, and folded it. The paper was a little damp, where a tear had fallen. But she felt better for having written it.

Hunt said, "Finished?"

"Yes, darling ... Would you like to see it?"

He took it from her, skimmed through it, grunted. "Yes, that should lessen the shock when they see you."

"I hope so. Have you got a stamp?"

He found one, and gave it to her.

"I could go and post it myself, couldn't I?" she said. "It doesn't really matter about me being seen now, does it? Anyway, it's dark. ..."

"Won't it do after we've been for our row? It won't go till to-morrow—and we're missing all the fine evening."

"I'd like to know it's in the box," she said. "Then I'll feel settled."

"Better give it to me, then—I'll be quicker." Hunt took the letter. "You get ready."

He walked to the office, let himself in, and put the letter in a file. He must remember to destroy it later. Also, the scribblings that Gwenda had left around in the cabin ... He stood at the site entrance long enough to cover the short two-way walk to the post box.

On the way back to the boat he collected the mahogany dinghy. It was larger than the green pram, much better for his purpose. He rowed to *Flavia*, and climbed aboard. "Ready?" he called.

"Just coming, darling."

He waited, fuming.

She emerged at last. "You'll have to do the rowing," she said. "I've got a blister."

"I'll be glad to," he said. "I need the exercise." He helped her down. For a moment he stood in the cockpit, listening. No human sounds were audible. A dog was barking in the village—an owl hooting across the fen—nothing else. ... In that wilderness of swamp and water beyond the lode, there'd be no interruptions. ...

He switched off the cabin lights and joined Gwenda in the dinghy. She untied the painter, and he pushed off.

"The water's quite warm," Gwenda said, dangling her fingers.

"Yes—it's all this sun. ..."

"Where are we going, darling?"

"Oh—along one of the dykes."

He turned off at the first junction with the lode, into a narrower channel between tall reeds. They seemed to be gliding now on a moonlit path. The only sounds that broke the silence were the faint rustle of the reeds, the splash of oars, and their own voices. If it hadn't been for the headlights through the village, they could have been a hundred miles from civilisation.

"Romantic, isn't it?" Gwenda said.

"Yes."

"I think I've been along this dyke before, but it looks so different at night. ... I've done a lot of rowing—I'll quite miss it. ..." She chattered on, happily. Hunt put in a word from time to time—but his thoughts were entirely on what he must do.

It would be unpleasant—he knew that. He wasn't a sadist. He

was just a man who wanted a fortune. Better not to dwell. Make it quick, when the moment came. His hands were strong, her throat was slim. . . . Watch out for those scratches. Kneel on her arms. . . . Afterwards, it wouldn't be so bad. Just hard work. He'd have to go back to the site for his gumboots and overalls. And Gwenda's belongings—all her clothes and things. They'd have to be buried, too. It would be quite a job—but he had the whole night before him . . . He mustn't forget the tidying up. The boat would have to be cleared of all traces—the dinghy checked over. Not that anyone would be interested now. But the time for safe mistakes was almost past. . . .

He turned into another dyke. Not much farther to go. . . . Sweat gathered on his forehead—but not from exertion. He found it almost impossible now to answer Gwenda's words and thoughts. When she laughed, in that lighthearted way of hers, it jarred horribly. Why didn't she shut up? God, what a time he'd had living in that boat with her. . . .! Well, it was nearly over. . . .

PART FOUR

Chapter One

For once, Dyson drove flat out, screeching round bends, racing along the straights, ruthlessly clearing the road ahead with horn and headlamps. Nield urged him on. In less than thirty minutes they were braking to a halt outside Hunt's office.

The silence of the place increased their fears. . . . Office in darkness, and locked. No light in Hunt's van. No light or sign of life anywhere. But the MG was parked beside the van—Hunt hadn't left by car. And if not by car . . .

Dyson stepped to the lode and shone his torch along it. "His dinghy's gone, sir."

Nield joined him. Together, they gazed out across the fen, over the moonlit reeds. Dyson's heart sank. All those hundred of acres of water and wilderness. They'd never find him in time. . . .

Then Nield had a flash of inspiration. He grabbed Dyson's arm. "Come on . . . Through the main entrance. . . . Quicker to drive."

He raced for the car, with Dyson at his heels. In a moment they were roaring out of the site, sweeping past the warden's cottage, parking by the gate. Nield was out of the car before it had stopped—and beginning to run. The younger man quickly overtook him.

"Don't wait for me," Nield shouted. "Make for—Stoker's Drove. . . ."

Stoker's Drove . . . ! Dyson rushed ahead. *Of course.* Where else . . .? He put on speed, running now as he'd never run before, following the path he knew. In a matter of minutes he reached the dyke. As he turned along the drove towards the bend, he thought he heard voices. He stopped for a second to listen, to check the direction. Yes—voices ahead. . . . And another sound—waterborne, clear, unmistakable . . .! The laughter of a girl . . . They were in time after all. . . .

He raced on. A hundred yards to the bend now. . . . Suddenly a new sound reached him—a sound that almost froze his blood. A gay laugh, cut off in mid-course. Then a choking, stifled scream. . . .

Dyson shouted—a warning shout at the full pitch of his lungs. He was almost there. He rounded the bend and shouted again, waving his torch. In a moment he spotted the dinghy. It was tied up on the outside of the working punt. Gwenda was lying across a thwart, limp and motionless, her hair streaming in the bilge. Hunt was half standing, gazing in the direction of the shout. A second later he was across the punt and leaping ashore. By his posture, he was going to fight. Dyson braced himself for the collision. Then, as Hunt recognised Dyson, he suddenly turned and began to run. Dyson dropped the torch, hurled himself forward in a flying tackle, grabbed a leg, and brought his man down with a thud.

A confused and savage struggle followed. Dyson was tough and trained, but badly winded from his run; Hunt was heavier and more powerful. In the poor light, accuracy was impossible. They rolled together in the mire of the path, punching, clawing and jabbing at anything they could find. Only a chance blow, or exhaustion, could settle it. Once they rolled heavily over the iron spike to which the punt was moored, and Hunt took the punishment. Dyson, in his fury, was scarcely aware of pain, or of the blood that was trickling down into his eyes.

Then, as they squirmed in the slippery mud, Hunt managed to break free. It was what he'd been trying to do all along—flight was his last, slender hope. He scrambled to his feet. Dyson, up in the same instant, suddenly sensed a light along the path. Nield. . . . Encouraged, he rushed forward and delivered a tremendous right-hand swing at the retreating shadow—and, by luck, connected with something hard. Hunt staggered. Dyson was carried on by his own momentum. Before he could check his rush he tripped on the mooring spike, somersaulted over the punt and dinghy and fell, headlong into the dyke. As he fell, he clutched the gunwale of the dinghy and it overturned.

He came up gasping. He heard a shout—Nield yelling "Get the girl!" He needed no telling. He looked wildly around. The surface of the water was unbroken. He plunged his head down, trying to see. The thick ooze at the bottom had been stirred up, and visibility was nil. All he could do was feel. He groped around desperately, half walking in the waist-deep water, half swimming . . . She couldn't be far away—there was almost no current . . . Then he touched something. Clothing . . . An arm . . . In a moment, he had dragged her to the bank. It had taken only seconds. . . .

He was just in time to witness a tableau he would never afterwards forget. Hunt, falling back, felled to the ground. Nield, standing over him with the spade he'd snatched from the punt. . . .

It seemed at first that Gwenda had been saved from strangling, only to die by misadventure in the muddy water of the dyke. Lying there white in the moonlight with her hair spread round her head like tangled weed, she looked a drowned Ophelia. Dyson couldn't believe it. He flung himself down and went at once into the practised routine of the "kiss of life" . . . Approach from the side—girl's head pressed back and held with both his hands—nostrils obstructed with his cheek—her mouth sealed with his own—watch for the chest to rise. . . . Almost at once, he got results. Gwenda gasped and started to breathe spontaneously. Back to a shuddering consciousness, back to life. . . .

Nield stayed with her while Dyson dragged the half-submerged dinghy from the water, drained it, and recovered the oars from the reeds downstream. The sergeant appeared to be having trouble with his right hand. "I'll row," Nield said. "You take the girl in the stern." Dyson sat down, and Nield lifted Gwenda and passed her to him. "Put this round her," he said, peeling off his jacket. Then he went back for Hunt. . . .

It was a nightmare journey through the fen—short in distance, but seemingly infinite in time. Dyson, soaked and battered, sat nursing Gwenda, now fully conscious and groaning with pain. He could do nothing for her except hold her close, speak soothingly, tell her it was all right now, that she'd soon be warm and comfortable. Hunt, stretched out on the floorboards, was breathing stertorously, with blood oozing from his head. Nield closed his mind to the sounds and concentrated on his rowing. . . .

The site at last . . . Now both policemen went quickly and efficiently into action. Dyson carried Gwenda to Hunt's caravan, forced the door, lit the gas fire, helped her out of her wet clothes, and wrapped her in blankets. Nield rang for a doctor and ambulance from Newmarket. Dyson changed into an outfit of Hunt's, and then made hot, sweet tea, laced with whisky. He tried to give Gwenda a little, but she couldn't swallow. She lay holding her throat, crying weakly. . . .

The minutes dragged like hours before the ambulance came. Then, inexpressible relief, as fresh, competent men took over. A stretcher for Gwenda, and the doctor's care. A second journey, to pick up Hunt from the dinghy. . . .

"You'd better go with them," Nield told Dyson. "I'll bring the car . . . Get yourself fixed up—that finger of yours looks broken. Then get along home. I'll see you to-morrow."

Nield made a couple of telephone calls after the ambulance had left. One to headquarters, to report the outcome of the case. Another to the Peterborough police, asking them to get in touch with Gwenda's parents. "Tell them she's safe but ill," he said, "and offer them transport to the hospital. Nothing else . . . I'll see them there and explain everything."

Afterwards, he made a tour of the site. Even though he knew that Gwenda had stayed there, it took him a little while to discover where. But he came in the end to *Flavia*, with its revealing contents. Gwenda's clothes and belongings. The many signs of double occupation. The fading chrysanthemums . . . What a nerve the fellow had had!

On the cabin table, he found the pathetic false starts of Gwenda's letter to her parents. . . . It was only later he learned that the letter had been written that evening—and that by writing it, Gwenda had saved her life. . . .

Chapter Two

Nield was late getting to headquarters next morning. The ordeal of the night, and particularly the unaccustomed running in the fen, had left him stiff and tired ... Dyson was even later. He arrived about eleven, with a bandaged right hand and a swathed right eye—though the uncovered eye had a cheerful gleam.

"Morning, sir ... How's Gwenda?"

"She's going to be all right," Nield said. "Her throat's still painful but there's no serious damage. Hunt must have been stopped by your shout before he really put the pressure on—they think the girl fainted from shock. A near thing, though ..."

Dyson nodded.

"By the way," Nield said, "she's had a miscarriage ... Not surprising, after all she went through."

Dyson was silent for a moment. "Well, I shouldn't think she'd have wanted the child, would she?—not now ... That fellow's a monster."

"Yes. ..."

"Are her parents with her?"

"Yes—they got there in the early hours. I had a session with them after they'd seen her. They've certainly learned a lot about life in the last few days ... But they're all right—they're good people. ..."

Dyson nodded again. "And how's Hunt?"

"As well as can be expected," Nield said grimly. "Considering he was arrested with the flat of a spade. ... Fractured skull—but he'll recover."

"What exactly happened, sir?"

"Well," Nield said, "I came pounding up just after you'd socked him. He was groggy, but recovering . . . I knew I couldn't manage him without you, if he fought, or catch him if he ran—and I'd no breath left for the water. So I grabbed the spade and cracked it down on his head. I was afraid we might lose them both."

"I thought we *had* lost the girl," Dyson said. "I'll never forget those few moments—groping around in the muck."

"You did well, Sarge—then and earlier. . . . It was your case—and I shall say so."

"It was you who thought of Stoker's Drove," Dyson said.

"Well, yes . . . It suddenly came to me—where else would he have planned to take her but the place he'd already got us to dig up . . . I must say it was a brilliant scheme—getting the search over first. If things hadn't gone wrong for him, we'd never have looked there again."

"The whole damned plot was brilliant," Dyson said. "A trial run, eh . . .? What will he get for his cleverness—ten years?"

"For attempted murder and grievous bodily harm . . .? More, I should think,"

Dyson grunted. "Have you been in touch with Ainger?"

"Yes, I phoned him this morning."

"Pretty rough on that poor kid, too."

"You're right," Nield said. "A lucky escape for her, of course—but I don't suppose that's much consolation at the moment . . . Hunt's left a lot of debris."

Dyson nodded slowly. That was the word—debris. Human debris . . . He thought of Gwenda—young, impressionable, deeply in love with a man, carrying his child—and then the hideous shock, the unbelievable assault—. . . . Would she ever get over it? It was bad enough when violence was accidental. Dyson knew plenty about that. The shattering horror—and the emptiness . . . How much worse when the violence was deliberate. How much harder the recovery. . . .

He looked at Nield. "What's the form now, sir? Are we still on duty?"

"I am, Sarge, till I've sent my report in . . . You're on sick leave. Super's orders."

"Good . . . Then I think I'll take a run over to Newmarket and see how Gwenda's getting on."

Nield smiled. "Going to try another kiss of life, Tom?"

"Who knows?" Dyson said.